## PROLOGUE

"We embrace evil and welcome it into our hearts. Lord of Darkness and Despair, please accept our sacrifice and grace us with your presence tonight."

Leah's ominous words hung in the air, her entire body trembling with anticipation, nerves on fire. As if to lend weight to the disturbing mantra, lightning bathed her one-bedroom downtown Los Angeles apartment in a sickly glow. Thunder rattled the windows, and the black candles hissed and flickered, painting surreal shadows over the circle of spiritual adventurers who'd gathered in her living room on this stormy summer evening. They were friends from college, philosophy and art students with open minds and raging hearts eager to explore the dark mysteries of the great beyond.

*Fools dabbling with forces they don't understand and will never be able to control.*

The thought came unbidden, almost as if some invisible entity had momentarily invaded Leah's mind.

Leah clenched her jaw and silenced the voice of doubt, which sounded so much like her ex. Screw Sean. The cocky bastard had made fun of her interest in the supernatural any chance he could. She should have known that dating a first-year engineering student wouldn't turn out well. Materialist jerk! Their recent break-up had driven her even deeper into her weird hobby.

To be honest, deep down she didn't really believe in magic. But she wanted to.

Leah wished to shatter her mundane everyday reality and inject a sense of wonder into her boring, humdrum life. Even though none of her spells and rituals had ever worked in the past, she still loved dabbling in the dark arts.

Determined to complete the ritual, she commenced the Latin portion of the incantation. Her friends joined in, their collective voices building into a hypnotic chorus. They had rehearsed the next part of the ceremony for weeks. Hopefully their hard work would pay off.

She held up a flame-shaped dagger and drew the sharp end across her palm, drawing blood. Biting her lip, she let a few drops fall into a highly adorned silver chalice. She wiped the blade clean with a black towel and handed the dagger to the Goth kid sitting next to her. One by one, the

# NIGHT SLAYER

## MIDNIGHT WAR

### WILLIAM MASSA

CRITICAL MASS PUBLISHING

Copyright © 2018 by WILLIAM MASSA

All rights reserved.

No part of this book may be reproduced in any form or by any electronic or mechanical means, including information storage and retrieval systems, without written permission from the author, except for the use of brief quotations in a book review.

Cover Design: Raul Ferran/NeoStock

other five people in the circle followed her example. By the time the cup returned to her, it was half full.

*Accept our sacrifice.*

Outside, lightning raked the sky, and thunder exploded, spurring her on.

They all held up their bloody hands now in a silent salute, allowing themselves to become one organism filled with a singular intent—to greet the darkness.

Words flowed faster over Leah's lips, and the group's chanting grew louder.

Was a note of desperation already creeping into their sing-song chant? Acceptance that their spell was falling on deaf ears? That in the end, despite all the black clothing and occult paraphernalia, it was all just a game?

*No!*

*I open my heart to the darkness...*

There was another loud crack, but it wasn't thunder this time. The sound had come from the wall in front of her.

Leah's heart beat hard against her rib cage, excitement mixing with growing terror. It was working!

A fissure split the wall behind the big screen TV.

Heads whipped around, eyes widened with shocked surprise. "Don't break the circle!" Leah cried as the person nearest to the wall tried to jerk away.

The cracks zig-zagged over the full length of the living room's wall, sending clouds of plaster into her nostrils and lungs. She fought back a cough. The apartment hummed with electricity, and the temperature jumped up by at least ten degrees as a ghostly green light bled through the expanding cracks. A foul stench weighed down the stale air, an odor of rotten meat, mold and decay.

Her friends froze with terror, lips still mouthing the incantation while their eyes fixed on the pulsating cracks across the wall. And then the wall split in two, parting like the two halves of a doorway between worlds. Phosphorescent clouds spilled into Leah's apartment and...

A humanoid shape grew visible in the widening vortex of paranormal light.

*Magic is real, Sean. Told you so.*

The thought sent a dark thrill through her, but the feeling soon turned to horror.

A bestial shriek announced the arrival of the supernatural being. The *thing* emerged from the jagged hole in the crumbling wall, its pale, glistening limbs crowding into the cramped apartment. There was no beauty to this monstrous being, no grace or elegance. Part emaciated hag, albino-white skin stretched over jagged bones, and part scaly reptile, the demon radiated menace...and hunger. Razor-sharp teeth clacked and saliva drooled as its skeletal arms extended toward the horrified crowd of wannabe occultists.

Leah's voice shook and sweat beaded her forehead as

she said, "Don't break contact, keep holding hands or the demon will be able to escape from the binding circle."

Her panicky eyes fixed on the pentagram she'd drawn on the floor earlier. It had lit up with an otherworldly light, now transformed into a swirling vortex of power that bathed their faces in a spectral glow.

The beast regarded them for a beat and then unleashed a bellowing shriek that sent the insides of Leah's stomach up into her throat. With mounting terror she watched as two of her friends wrenched their hands free and jumped to their feet, conquered by their own fear, and now stood outside the broken binding circle.

The demon twitched.

That was all the warning they were to receive. The creature's clawed hand slashed out and removed half of Leah's face with an almost lazy flick of its wrist. As she slumped forward, a final thought slashed through her mind: *What have we done?*

The answer was simple—they'd made a fatal mistake.

Her friends were about to find out that black magic was all too real.

That the darkness was armed with teeth and claws.

And it was very hungry.

# 1

The LAPD SWAT truck barreled through traffic with alarming speed, sirens at full tilt. My gloved hand tightened around the HK MP5 9mm submachine gun strapped to my chest as we rocketed into a turn.

Joe, our driver, must've been a street racer in a former life. Besides myself, nine more SWAT officers filled up the back of the claustrophobic truck. Their solemn faces mirrored my own under their helmets, aviator shades, and bulky Kevlar vests—frozen warrior statues who would spring to lethal life once we arrived at our destination. Their weapons gleamed in the moonlight trickling through the truck's windows.

I would have trusted every one of these superbly trained professionals with my life.

After all, this was my team.

My name is Jason Night. I'm thirty-one, a former Marine, and proud to be the commander of this group of elite law enforcement officers.

Despite the sickening levels of violence I've encountered over the years, my stomach churned with anxiety at the thought of what might be waiting for us downtown. I hated walking into a situation with sketchy intel. Or, in this case, practically nonexistent intelligence. This much was known at this point: chaos had erupted around 9:25 pm in a six-floor residential building that mostly housed USC students. Neighbors reported hearing both screams and shots; there was even one eyewitness account of a resident plunging six stories to their death.

The first cops on the scene had bravely entered the building. Within minutes, their radios had gone silent. History repeated itself when the next wave of cops arrived. According to the panicked voices buzzing over our headsets, the building seemed to swallow up anyone who was foolish enough to set foot inside.

The time had come for SWAT to turn things around and break that disturbing pattern.

"What are we walking into here, Sergeant?"

The question had come from Tia, the only woman in the squad. She wasn't here to fill some political quota–the bulging biceps beneath her tactical gear and the calm strength in her eyes quickly shut up any fool willing to doubt her credentials.

"Based on the available intel, it's most likely an active shooter scenario."

"Have there been any demands or evidence of hostages?" Taylor asked. He was twenty-eight, a former Navy SEAL who was built like an ox.

I shook my head. "All attempts to reach anyone inside the building have failed."

"So we have no idea what we're up against here?"

*Couldn't have put it better, bud*, I thought. But unlike regular cops, we were sporting considerably more firepower and would show zero hesitation to use it at the first signs of violence.

The truck slowed. It was time to get this party started.

I was up and out the door as soon as the vehicle ground to a halt, Tia just a step behind.

Weeks of oppressive heat had finally exploded in a thunderstorm, a rarity for Los Angeles. Thankfully it had stopped raining even though flashes of lightning still lit up the dark night sky and peals of thunder shredded the air.

One by one we emerged from the truck, submachine guns leveled and ready as our black combats boots slapped the wet asphalt. I had expected to see a crowd of curious onlookers, but this was downtown LA after a rainstorm, and the slick streets were deserted. As we cut through the night, I took note of the three police cruisers and two ambulances parked in front of the apartment building. The sound of crackling radios filled the air, but no one was around to answer the incoming calls, the vehicles sat abandoned.

I scanned the area and finally spotted a single police officer who slouched forlornly among the flashing sirens, red and blue lights washing over blood-caked features.

I approached the cop with quick steps. "What happened? Are you okay?" I shouted while I nodded at one of my men to take a closer look at the cop's injuries.

His thousand-yard stare didn't acknowledge our presence. The man was in shock.

What the hell was happening inside that building?

I shifted my attention to the looming structure before us. Moonlight played over the steel and glass tower. As lightning webbed the sky high above, I was gripped by a feeling of foreboding, an unshakable sense that whatever was waiting for us inside, it would be unlike anything I'd ever encountered before.

I'm not superstitious, in fact, my ex used to say I was skeptical to a fault, but I usually trust my hunches.

I should have listened to my instincts this time.

I stole a quick glance at the shadowy main entrance and decided it might be wiser to enter the building from the rear. The direct approach didn't seem to be working

My men fell in step with me, and we advanced toward the right side of the building where an alley ran along the back of the structure. We rounded a collection of dumpsters overflowing with trash and soaked cardboard boxes and made our way toward a heavy steel door.

As we drew closer to the rear entrance, I noticed a bearded, trench-coat wearing figure slouched on the pavement. Just one more homeless bum sleeping off his latest bender. Downtown Los Angeles was full of these lost souls.

A wave of alcohol and body odor wafted from the unconscious figure. I gagged at the stench but also felt bad for the guy. Hopefully, one day in the future, the city would get their act together and find a better solution than letting these poor people fend for themselves.

Turning away from the vagrant, I gave Rodney the hand signal to start picking the steel door's lock.

At twenty-five, he was the youngest member of my team, but his grey eyes and chiseled intensity made him look a lot older. My radio hissed and crackled as rainwater bubbled down a storm drain behind me, making it hard to hear if anything was moving on the other side of the door.

I took measured breaths as Rodney worked his magic, intent on steadying my nerves and centering myself.

*This is taking too damn long.*

Almost as if to lend weight to the thought, a bloodcurdling scream pierced the night. It was followed by the sound of breaking glass. I glanced upward and saw a young man in a Lakers jersey pounding the window on the fifth floor, tattooing the glass with bloody handprints.

I traded an alarmed look with my team. Then I glanced

at Frank. At six foot three, he was the tallest man in the team.

"We need to get in there now!"

Frank nodded, and his trunk-sized arms leveled a breaching shotgun at the door. He depressed the trigger, and with a deafening *KABOOM*, a series of shock-lock slugs shattered the hinges.

I raised a boot and kicked the door open. A beat later I was inside the building, moving, moving.

The scream had proven one thing to me. There were still innocent lives at stake here. I had a sickening sense that we'd arrive too late to save the man in the basketball jersey, but there might be others. Hiding from the killer or killers rampaging through the building, desperately praying for help to arrive in time.

*We're here now*, I thought, wishing I could telepathically communicate with any survivors.

*Hold on just a little longer. We'll get you out of this place.*

I charged down the hallway with quick precision, my team right behind me.

And then I froze.

A scene out of a horror movie awaited us in the building's main lobby. Two dead cops and one EMT worker lay sprawled on the stone floor in widening pools of red. Crouched over one of the corpses was a young Asian man, barely college age, his face still covered in acne. His mouth was rimmed in red as he lapped up the blood on the floor.

He whirled toward me with a hiss, his glaring eyes green slits.

*What the fuck?*

Displaying animalistic grace, the Asian kid sprang to his feet. And that's when I spotted the knife in his crimson hand. As he leaped at me, jaws snapping like a rabid animal, I instinctively squeezed the trigger. The burst from my MP-5 submachine gun slammed into his body, the impact sending him into a wall of mailboxes.

I noticed the blood spatter on my black vest, and icy horror gripped me. Fuck, I'd seen way too many zombie movies over the years. I hoped to God that whatever madness had seized the kid wasn't contagious. This wasn't some hostage rescue situation anymore but a scene straight out of a nightmare.

"Holy shit!" Frank exclaimed. The man had witnessed his fair share of crazy and didn't spook easily. But cannibalism was a new one for both of us.

I weaved past the downed bodies and approached the kid who had tried to take a bite out of me. He was down, dying but still clinging to life despite the bullets I had pumped into him. His eyes regarded me with contempt as he started shouting in a foreign language at me.

"Anyone know what language that is?" Tia asked.

"Latin," I said. I couldn't understand what he was saying, but years of attending both Catholic school and mass allowed me to at least recognize the language. Things were getting stranger by the minute.

Another shriek cut through the lobby and we all turned toward the staircase. The demented cries had emanated from a few floors above us. Unlike the terrified scream we had heard in the alley, these shrieks barely sounded human. Were there more of these crazies in the building?

Eyeing the Asian kid as he let out his final gasp, I wondered what could turn a young college kid into a cannibalistic terror. Drugs? Some kind of disease? Whatever was happening here, it needed to end. Now.

I nodded at my team, who all looked pale but determined, and we rushed up the stairs in tight formation, climbing one flight after another. I could practically smell our fear, but we were professionals. As long as innocent lives were at stake, we had to press on, no matter how crazy the situation might be.

My stomach churned as more bestial shrieks filled the stairway. Lips pressed into a thin line, jaw set, I let the chilling sounds guide me. When I reached the third floor, I finally spotted another one of the possessed freaks. This one was female and dressed all in black, a goth girl on steroids, tats and piercings wherever there was bare skin. She might've been pretty once upon a time before the madness had taken over.

The young woman snarled at me, her eyes wide with rage and hatred.

I swallowed hard. This girl sported the same inhumanly black gaze as the Asian kid downstairs. Her face was masked in gore, more like a ravenous beast on the prowl than a human being. She emitted a monstrous howl and dove down the stairs right at us.

Tia reacted first and fired. The barrage of lead sent the goth girl over the railing and on a three-story dive to the lobby below. A muffled thump reverberated through the staircase as she smashed into the stone floor below.

This was turning into a massacre. Shit, the press would have a field day—heavily armed SWAT team mowing down unarmed students wouldn't play well on the news. I could almost see the headlines.

"What the hell are these kids on?" Rodney said, his voice shaky. "Could it be meth or bath salts?"

I recalled the story of a drug addict, high on so-called bath salts, who had chewed a homeless man's face off in Miami. Is that what had transformed regular college kids into blood-thirsty monsters? Anything was possible in the crazy world we lived in nowadays.

I pushed back my dark thoughts and pressed onward.

Reaching the fourth floor I peered down the corridor, first to my right and then to my left. Hallways stretched into darkness on both ends.

All clear.

I was about to climb the next flight of stairs when I saw waves of green light radiating from one of the doors at the far end of the hallway to my right.

"What the hell is that?" Frank asked.

No one ventured a guess or offered up some half-baked theory, our attention focused on the glowing hallway.

I shrugged. There was only one way to find out.

I made a quick decision and eyed Tia and Frank. "You two are with me." I turned to Taylor and the others. "Stay here, but keep your guard up. Make sure no one sneaks up on us from behind."

Frank nodded and said, "You got it, boss."

"We'll be back in a minute."

With these words, I rushed down the hallway, Tia and Frank right behind me, determined to get to the bottom of the mystery.

As I closed in on the glowing doorway, I spotted more corpses. Lifeless eyes fixed into nothingness, lives struck down in their prime. I'd seen too many dead kids, lost too many friends, in two wars. At least the Marines I'd fought beside had sacrificed their lives for a cause they believed in, warriors and heroes. These dead College kids were just collateral damage. Dammit, what a waste.

My throat tightened with growing anger. When I found who did this, they would pay.

My MP5 leveled, gloved hand ready to squeeze the trigger, I reached the strangely glowing door. Ghostly light washed over the visor of my helmet as I cautiously entered the apartment. The eerie light was everywhere, and an instinctive, primal part of me wanted to turn on my heels and run.

*Don't go into the light, Carol Anne.* The line from *Poltergeist* echoed through my mind as I kept setting one foot in front of the other. Only my training was preventing me from taking off in the other direction.

The glowing light was blinding, and I blinked a few times. Finally, my vision adjusted and details jumped into view. Bodies lay sprawled across the apartment's living room floor in pools of gore.

My right eye started to twitch. That generally happens when bad shit goes down. And this was a textbook example of *bad shit*. I hadn't encountered such a grisly sight since dealing with IEDs back in Iraq.

My gaze traveled from the bodies to the glowing five-pointed star etched into the living room floor. The pentagram appeared to be the source of the spectral light.

What sort of fucked up ritual had these kids performed in here? And why the hell was the symbol glowing like that? I didn't see any blacklights.

I edged closer, gun ready for the slightest hint of movement or provocation of any kind. I was almost itching for a confrontation.

"What is all this shit?" Tia said, unable to hide the fear in her voice as her gloved hand touched the crucifix she wore around her neck at all times. I wished I had an explanation for the madness, but I didn't. None of this made sense.

My pulse quickened as I continued to search the apartment. Further inspection of the place revealed all kinds of funky occult paraphernalia. An overturned chalice sticky with blood and an ancient looking dagger rested outside the circle. The walls were lined with books on witchcraft and ceremonial magic, the titles peppered with disturbing keywords such as *Maleficarum* and *Daemon*. Not exactly light summer beach reading.

A clap of thunder erupted outside, and even the toughest among us flinched.

"This is nuts," Frank said.

"You think the people who attacked us were part of some cult?" Tia asked.

I considered this possibility. I mentally played back the attacks, focusing on the details in my mind. The inhuman expression in my assailants' eyes had rattled me to the core. Back in Iraq, I'd seen real evil, and I knew from years of experience what fanatics looked like. But I'd never encountered anything like those two rabid college kids before.

No, this was different. Worse.

My attention returned to the occult collection in the apartment. If not for the dead bodies, it would have all seemed pretty ridiculous to me. But then there was the matter of the glowing pentagram. Phosphorescent light enveloped my team and me as we drew closer to the eerie circle. I crouched over the shimmering symbol, hoping to gain a better understanding of what I was looking at.

But the answers would have to wait as muffled gunfire rolled into the creepy apartment. It was coming from the hallway.

I swapped a look with Tia and Frank.

The team was in trouble.

# 2

We retraced our steps down the hallway, weapons ready. The air was thick with the smell of cordite and copper.

"What the hell is going on out there?" I shouted into my mic.

The only answer was hissing static.

Moments later, Tia, Frank, and I reached the landing where we had left the rest of the team.

At first, I couldn't understand what I was looking at. It was like a bomb had gone off, reducing my team to piles of Kevlar soaked in gore.

"Oh, Jesus, oh my God..." Taylor stammered, verbalizing what we were all thinking.

I stepped toward the elevators, my boots leaving bloody footprints on the landing's cheap carpet as I tried to make sense of what my mind refused to accept. My men were dead. All seven of them. It couldn't be. I knew these people better than I knew myself, spent almost every day with them, trained and tested them. They were the best of the best, the elite, the LAPD's tip of the spear.

But more importantly, they were my family. Just the other day, we had all let off some steam at Moe's, a cop bar near the precinct. There had been laughs and beers and...

I choked up.

They were all gone.

Shock gripped me, and icy waves of dread spiked up my spine.

Who could sneak up on a SWAT team? The crazies who had attacked us posed a threat, but they were no match for the firepower of my team. So who could have done this?

*"They did it,"* a female voice hissed. I whirled, blood roaring in my ears. Where had the mystery voice come from? My eyes bored into the encroaching darkness.

*"Tia and Frank. They betrayed you! And now they will kill you too!"*

I swallowed hard. This time there was no doubt—the voice wasn't emanating from the adjacent corridors. The voice was inside of me.

*"Act now before it's too late! Shoot them before they can shoot you!"*

I whirled toward Tia and Frank. They were both raising their MP-5s at each other. A part of me wanted to do the same, to kill them before these treacherous bastards could gang up on me. But the rational part of my mind, the man who trusted my team members implicitly, refused to heed the persuasive call for violence.

"*Fool! They will kill you,*" the shrill voice shouted. "*Destroy the bastards before they can destroy you!*"

No...

I raised my MP5, hands shaking.

*You have to fight this*, I told myself over and over again. *FIGHT IT!*

A scream erupted from my throat as I emptied a full magazine into the nearest wall. Bullets chopped mortar. Plaster and smoke choked the air. The *click-click* of my finger reflexively depressing the trigger echoed like a metronome in the hallway.

I had stopped myself. But Tia and Frank weren't so lucky. They brought up their submachine guns and fired at each other. Bullets shredded their body armor and found the unprotected flesh below. Blood sprayed as they both went down.

Driven by pure instinct, my training taking over, I ejected the empty magazine and replaced it. Numb to the core, I advanced, gun pointed at the floor in case I succumbed to the incessant whispers in my head. Even though Tia and Frank were already down, a part of me wanted to join the killing and unload my weapon at my fellow SWAT officers. I had never felt anything like this dark compulsion before.

"*Do it,*" the voice urged. "*You failed them. You let them die. Turn the gun on yourself.*"

Those were not my thoughts. What was happening to me?

A sound above me momentarily provided a distraction from this latest horror. My head turned toward the landing's ceiling, and my breath hitched in my throat.

A woman was looking down at me from above. She stood suspended, upside down, unaffected by gravity. The sun-kissed beauty was naked, her almond-shaped blue eyes locked on me. A mane of straw-colored hair spilled down her shoulders and pointed toward the ceiling, not the floor, defying the laws of gravity and physics. Her breasts were perfect, the golden skin of her curvaceous thighs inviting. She was both a vision and a nightmare, and I couldn't take my eyes off her.

The interest appeared to be mutual. The woman licked her lips and shifted slightly, beckoning me.

I heard a sound behind me, and a second later, there was a deafening boom, followed by the sensation of a monstrous force slamming into me as bullets pockmarked my Kevlar vest. The impact sent me flying, and I crashed to the ground, the dead bodies of my slaughtered team members staring back at me from every angle.

More bullets ricocheted around me, and I crawled on

my belly in a desperate attempt to escape the gunfire. Two shots missed me, but the third one crashed again into my vest, sending a renewed burst of pain into my chest.

My gaze landed on Tia. She was on the ground, her face a scarlet mask twisted with homicidal rage, the barrel of her submachine leveled at me. She must have been barely clinging to life, but apparently Tia was determined to use her dying breaths to end me.

Fuck, I had to get off the landing. Now.

Fueled by desperation, I hurled myself toward the red-streaked stairs. Bullets detonated around me as I rolled painfully down the concrete and metal steps. I wanted to scream but lacked the strength. Thankfully I was still wearing my helmet and armor, which offered some protection as I crashed down the staircase.

I finally came to an abrupt stop and stole a glance upward. I saw Tia peering down at me, her gaze empty. She had crawled all the way to the edge of the staircase, still trying to kill me even as she finally succumbed to her injuries.

For a moment, I wanted nothing more than to shut down. I was a Marine and a SWAT officer, but this was pushing me to my very limits.

*Get up. Run. Survive.* A voice inside of me spoke up. Not the eerie hiss that had invaded my mind, but something deeper, more authentic.

And I tried. I swear to God I tried.

Before I could haul myself to my feet, another figured stepped to the edge of the landing above me and peered down. It was the woman from the ceiling. She loomed over Tia's corpse, her features strangely serene, as if she existed beyond pesky human emotions. Once again, I couldn't help but notice how perfect the woman was. Six feet tall, her body both athletic and curvaceous, breasts firm yet soft, a thin film of perspiration trickling down her taut stomach, her sex inviting—

*Snap out it!* I scolded myself. How could I be thinking about sex at a time like this? This thing, whatever it was, had somehow wiped out my team by making us all turn on each other. I had no doubt that she was the source of the madness.

I fought back my attraction, sensing that this woman could affect thoughts in more ways than one.

*"Why do you resist me?"*

I shook as the question cut through my thoughts.

"Get the hell out of my head," I growled under my breath.

The naked vision started descending the stairs, her movements lithe and sensuous but also filled with malevolent intent. I tasted fear in the back of my throat. This woman was both a goddess and an angel of death.

And now she was coming for me.

I had to get the hell out of here.

One of Tia's bullets had torn into my arm, and the

wound was bleeding profusely. Blood loss could become a life-threatening problem as the seconds stretched into minutes. I desperately stumbled back to my feet, every part of my body screaming with agony, and that's when the naked goddess launched herself down the staircase.

A whistling sound cut overhead, and she landed right in front of me with superhuman grace. Before I could respond, her perfectly shaped arm snapped out at me, long-nailed fingers closing around my throat in a viselike grip. She effortlessly lifted me into the air, my booted feet dangling off the ground and kicking at thin air. She might look like she only weighed a hundred and twenty pounds, but she possessed the strength of goddamn sumo wrestler. I desperately gasped for air.

*"You're foolish to resist me, human!"*

"Go to hell," I spat, struggling to escape her grip.

*"Oh, it's far too late for that."*

Scales rolled over her perfect skin, her mesmerizing eyes narrowing into animalistic slits while horns exploded from her mane of untamed hair. Was this what she really looked like?

Despite the fear, pain and lack of oxygen, rage bubbled up in me.

This monster had wiped out my team. Murdered my family.

My rage exploded, and I reached for my Sig Sauer 9mm. With a snarl frozen on my lips, I brought up my handgun and pointed the pistol at the creature's head. Without hesitation, I pulled the trigger.

The unholy thing, whatever it was, let go of me with a bone-chilling shriek.

I crumpled to the ground but somehow kept on firing. She unleashed wails of pain (or was it mere irritation?) as I unloaded a full magazine. Black blood sprayed where my bullets pierced her scaly flesh. Good. I had never hated someone as much as I hated this thing. It had taken everybody I cared about away from me.

The moment of victory proved to be short-lived. As I desperately ejected the spent magazine and reloaded, the monstrous woman wiped the blood from her face, her expression of pain transforming into a diabolical smile as she licked her own black blood off her chin. One by one, her gaping wounds sealed themselves. She regarded me with a mixture of surprise and annoyance. And there was some other emotion in those soulless eyes.

*Fascination.*

I guess she didn't come across too many men who played hard to get.

As her damaged body continued to regenerate, I dragged myself toward the next staircase. One more floor to the exit. I didn't know if I would be safe outside the building, but I had to try.

At least that was my plan for a split second before the woman launched her next attack.

Her arm snaked out, and she slapped me aside. The momentum behind the assault sent me over the railing and one story down to the lobby. I heard a sound of crunching bones and felt my arm snap like a twig as I landed. My helmeted head collided with the floor and a tidal wave of pain rippled through my skeleton.

Before I could even speculate about the extent of my injuries, I heard more footsteps. A group of young college kids surrounded me. Judging by their blank expressions, these kids were all under the woman's spell. But unlike her, they were regular people, and bullets could stop them. I reached for my Sig Sauer 9mm and realized the gun was gone. I must've dropped it during my fall.

*Fuck...*

The next instant, the mad horde was upon me. Knives flashed, and cold steel sank into the unprotected parts of my body. Again and again, the attackers found their targets. I tasted copper and knew I would exhale my last breath on the blood-soaked lobby floor, the exit only a few feet away.

The mob clawed and bit me, knives sinking into the exposed parts of my anatomy. Shit, at this rate, the mob would tear me apart. I had to find a way out.

That's when my bloodshot gaze landed on the Sig Sauer. Only two feet separated me from the firearm. Without hesitation, moving on pure instinct, I made a mad scramble for the weapon. I gritted my teeth as I hurled myself at the gun.

I landed right next to the pistol, scooped it up in one fluid motion, and spun toward my ravenous attackers. I fired left and right, barely needing to aim. I knew I would soon run out of bullets.

With a roar that bubbled with blood, I got to my feet and staggered down the corridor which would lead me to the rear exit. I somehow reached the steel door that we'd entered through less than ten minutes earlier. The horde was right behind me, in hot pursuit, determined to not let their prey escape.

One thing was clear—once you entered the building, you didn't get to leave. At least not as yourself. This building belonged to the black-blooded beauty.

I threw my whole weight against the door. It opened with a resounding clang, and then I was out in the wet alley. The night air tasted delicious as I took a deep breaths. Blood seeped out of me onto the rain-drenched asphalt. God, I was in dire need of medical attention.

*C'mon, Marine. Get moving.*

The steel door behind me flew open, and the horde spilled into the alley, eyes flashing with murderous intent.

Tapping into a last reservoir of strength, I sprinted down the alley at full bore—which wasn't all that fast in my battered, hemorrhaging state. I was running on pure grit at this point.

I made it to the end of the alley, where another surprise was waiting for me. A male college kid armed with a sharp kitchen knife was lurking in a pool of shadows. I caught a flash of steel, and then the blade went through my chest. And this time there was no protective Kevlar to stop it. I exhaled blood, and spasms of agony seared my whole being.

I emptied the last two remaining bullets into my latest attacker and sent him sprawling back into the darkness.

The kitchen knife stuck from my chest as I hunched over. I sank to my knees, one hand tight around the knife handle, my fingers coated red. Reality swam out of focus, and I felt the night closing in on me. This was it. I had reached the end of the line.

And that's when I spotted the figure in a red monk's robe across the street, standing in the open doorway of a small church. Despite my grave injuries, I felt confused. I didn't recall that church being here when I'd first arrived on the scene. Then again, I had focused on the apartment more than the immediate surroundings.

The mysterious figure kept waving me forward.

*Run if you want to live!*

Was that another voice in my head or just an echo of my own thoughts?

I craned my neck and saw more possessed kids sprinting after me. Drawing whatever reserves I had left, I hobbled across the street toward the church, every part of my body screaming for mercy. The figure in the monk's robe melted back into the dark church almost as if I had imagined it. Even though there was no trace of the person who had called me, the chapel still represented a sanctuary, and I darted inside.

As soon as I set foot in the house of God, the large wooden doors slammed shut behind me. For a brief moment, I heard the kids slamming into the now-closed church doors like human battering rams. And then all sounds drained from the world. I stared at the door, wondering what had happened.

I shifted my focus to the insides of the chapel, took one step.

And froze.

Wherever I was, it sure as hell wasn't like any church I'd ever visited before.

I found myself in a giant, cathedral-like structure, hewn from rough stone, a cavernous, vaulted ceiling stretching hundreds of feet above me. How could the small chapel I had entered house such a vast interior space? Impossible. My mind was playing tricks as death closed in. This place was a castle, not a church.

For a second, I wondered if I might have already died. Was this my first glimpse of the afterlife? I quickly cast that silly thought aside. I was in too much pain to be dead already.

Giant columns ran down the length of the chamber

and guttering torches conjured grotesque shadows in the windowless space. There were no pews, crosses or statues of Saints, no sign that this place was affiliated with any religion I had ever heard of.

My psychological equilibrium off, my body pushed to the brink, I took another step and a wave of weakness hit me. The world tilted and slipped out of focus, and I collapsed in a string-cut sprawl.

I let go and accepted my death.

But someone had very different plans for me.

I didn't know it at the time, but I was about to be reborn.

# 3

Darkness threatened to sweep me away as every part of my body shut down. My injuries were pushing me to my physical limits, which sounded a lot better than the truth—I was dying.

My eyelids grew heavy. Unconsciousness at least promised relief from the pain. And then I caught a flicker of movement from the corner of my eye. Two robed figures peeled from the encroaching shadows like ghosts and hustled toward me.

Before I knew what was happening, they had grabbed my arms and began to drag me across the flagstone floor. I wouldn't have been able to resist them even if I'd wanted to. I was done for, barely clinging to consciousness. I didn't feel the cold stone as it scraped my back, didn't react to the bony fingers digging into my shoulders, didn't feel much of anything. The world had become a dream.

No, a nightmare.

The two shadowy figures stopped and brusquely yanked me to my feet. Agony flooded my injured body, and I clenched my teeth, stifling a scream. On the positive side, the rough treatment jerked me awake. Reality snapped into focus as I stared at the altar before me. Strange glyphs and runes had been etched into its rough-hewn stone surface, symbols that distantly seemed familiar. Not Christian or Muslim or any other religion I had encountered in my thirty-one years on this planet.

Before I could protest, the two robed figures unceremoniously lifted me into the air, one holding me by the shoulders while the second hooded apparition grabbed me by the legs. I felt disconnected from my body, unable to fight back. I tried to scream but lacked the strength, my parched lips unable to form any coherent words.

The monks slapped me down on the stone altar like I was just a piece of meat. I blinked, guttering torches shining down at me like the lights in an operating room. The hooded spooks loomed, their faces shrouded in shadows. My arm shot out at one of the monks, and I somehow managed to tear the hood away, revealing the face underneath.

Or lack thereof.

I gasped in horror. The thing towering over me had no discernible features, no eyes, or nose or mouth. I was looking up at a mannequin come to life.

*Calm yourself, Slayer,* a voice spoke up in my mind. *The sorceress will be with you shortly.*

I made an attempt to grab the faceless creature again, but an invisible force slammed me back to the altar, making me feel like a pinned insect. I was unable to move, an enormous weight pressing down on me.

The two featureless creatures vanished in the shadows. My blood ran, sticky and red, over the rough stone surface of the altar. Terror prevented me from passing out.

I filled my lungs and screamed, "Help me, please, someone, get me out of here! HELP!"

"Hush now. Don't be afraid!"

I paused, still terrified but grateful to hear a human voice in this accursed temple. I squinted but couldn't detect any sign of the mysterious speaker. I tried to twist my head in the direction of the voice but failed. An inexplicable force pulled me toward the altar, almost as if the slab of rock was exerting a form of magnetism over my shattered body.

"Who the hell are you? What the fuck is happening?"

"My name is Octurna. And I'm about to save your life, Jason Night."

The voice was both feminine and commanding, seductive yet strangely cold and removed.

I never heard the speaker approach. No footsteps or rustling of fabric gave her away. A shadow fell over me, and I was looking up at one of the most beautiful creatures

I had ever laid eyes on. The woman was in her late twenties with high cheekbones, jet-black hair, and porcelain skin. She wore a crimson robe slashed at the neck to reveal a glimpse of her tantalizing cleavage. Catlike green eyes stared down at me with a calculating expression.

"I have been waiting for someone like you for years," she said.

"Someone like me?" I asked in a strangled voice.

"You're dying." Octurna's voice was matter-of-fact, impassive. "You're strong, but all your skills and talents won't matter if you bleed out on my altar."

Hey, I couldn't argue with that logic.

"What the hell do you want from me?" I croaked.

"Your strength. Your loyalty." Octurna leaned closer, her gaze imploring. "Do you promise to serve me if I save your life? Will you be my warrior, Jason? My Slayer?"

My face contorted with anger. I had no idea what this woman was yammering on about. Maybe, considering my sorry condition, I should have agreed to any deal she was willing to offer. But I hated being pushed into a corner. Even when my life hung in the balance.

"Screw you," I croaked with the last of my strength.

To my surprise, a smile played over Octurna's face, and for a moment, she looked like she was flesh and blood and not some perfect sculpture come alive. "I like your fighting spirit, Jason. You had best hold on to that anger if you want to make it through the next hour."

Octurna's sensuous lips pressed into a thin line, her features narrowing with concentration. While she drew closer, her robe shifted around her graceful neck, revealing again the swell of two perfect breasts. I swallowed hard.

Delicate hands with long nails slipped over my blood-soaked SWAT uniform, caressed my battered body and found my wounds. The contact was electric, and it sent shivers up and down my spine despite my pain. With her touch, vitality returned to my body. With it, my anger came rushing back.

"Who the hell are you?" I demanded to know. "And who was that fucking monster who murdered my men?"

"You survived a battle with a low-level demon. A succubus conjured by children who had no idea what they were doing. Consider it your first glimpse of a far larger world."

I shook my head. "I don't understand. What are you talking about?"

"The answers are coming. Patience, slayer."

Her finger brushed over the knife wound in my chest, and the pierced flesh reknitted itself. The throbbing pain subsided, and as the hole sealed up, the bleeding stopped. More injuries remained but this woman—witch, sorceress, goddess, or all of the above—could save me as long as I gave her what she wanted.

*Do you promise to serve me if I save your life?*

"What are you? Are you like the thing I faced in the

building?"

A wan smile played over Octurna's features in response to my question. "No. I'm very much human."

"How are you doing this?"

"Magic."

"I don't understand..."

"You will soon enough. Magic is beauty and ecstasy and power. Without it, the world would be devoid of miracles." She leaned closer and whispered into my ear. "I'm sorry about what happened to your friends. They were good people. Warriors. But you're more than that, Jason. You're a survivor."

She brushed her fingers delicately along my broken arm, sending shivers of delight through my body. I could feel the pain lifting, the bone resetting itself. My mind was reeling.

"Your men were disciplined, trained, well-armed, but they came up against an enemy they didn't understand."

Octurna's hands now found the bullet wound in my other arm. Her finger disappeared in the hole in my flesh, but there was no pain, almost as if her touch had an anesthetic effect on me. A moment passed, and she fished out the metal fragment and tossed it carelessly aside.

"What if I told you their deaths weren't in vain, that this terrible encounter served a higher purpose? Their sacrifice brought you to me."

I stared at her with a mixture of incomprehension and

anger. "Sacrifice? That goddamn witch slaughtered them!"

Her eyes flickered with a trace of irritation. Octurna clearly wasn't used to being addressed in such a tone. But who could blame me? I'd been to Hell and back, and my patience was running thin.

Her face relaxed, but her eyes continued to simmer. "There are other creatures like the succubus out there. Monsters who live in the shadows, biding their time. The demon you faced was a low-level thug. Imagine what the real nightmares are like. Think of how many innocent lives will perish in the future unless we stop the Shadow Cabal."

"What are you talking about?"

"I'm talking about vengeance. What would you give if I could help you destroy the monster who wiped out your team? Would you seize the opportunity to even the score, to make it suffer as much as its innocent victims?"

"Yes." The answer rolled off my tongue without hesitation.

"Good. Then we have an agreement, Jason Night."

As if to accentuate her point, Octurna waved both her hands over my body. Crackling tendrils of red light forked around her fingers and engulfed my chest. Within seconds, my remaining wounds sealed themselves. I was back to normal. Still superglued to the stone altar, but alive.

"You're brave and strong, Jason," Octurna said, "but the things you'll be going up against, well, it takes more than a broad back to battle the demons and their twisted masters."

I was struggling with what Octurna was telling me. Masters? Creatures of the night? My mind was going into overload. I never got a chance to give voice to the myriad of questions cycling through my mind as Octurna pulled out a flask. Before I could protest, she popped the cork from the flask and poured red liquid right into my open mouth. The red substance hit my lips and burned down my gullet. This sure as hell wasn't wine. The coppery swill made me gag.

"Dragon Blood will make you stronger, faster, less prone to injury."

The red stuff was still sizzling down my throat as the full meaning of Octurna's words hit me. She was making me drink blood? Could this nightmare get any stranger?

The answer was a resounding yes as Octurna started to remove her robe.

The fabric fell to the stone floor next to the altar.

I stifled a gasp. I had dated my fair share of women over the years, but the one in front of me was an erotic vision. Her flawless skin the color of marble, an intricate web of tattoos running across her whole body, delineating her breasts from her shoulders and surrounding her sex, forming fine-lined patterns which reminded me of crop circles. Instead of disfiguring her sensual beauty, the ink heightened it.

An almost irrational desire for this woman gripped me, and my body stirred.

"You will require more than just the right weapons to hunt creatures of darkness, Jason Night. You will have to *become* a weapon."

Her hands crackled with bluish flames, and the remainders of my blood-soaked black SWAT uniform evaporated into thin air. I was naked now my muscular body splayed out on a stone altar like a sacrifice to some mad god.

Or a goddess.

"You will need my strength. My magic is weak and depleted. I'm but a shadow of who I once was, but I'll share what little I have with you, Jason. Accept the power I'm about to gift you and make it your own."

Every cell in my body felt energized with desire despite all that had happened in the last hour. Octurna leaned forward, her breasts firm yet luscious, tantalizingly within reach. I wanted to cup those beauties and close my lips around her erect nipples. But even though she had healed my wounds, I remained like a statue.

Like some sleek jungle cat, my savior slipped onto the altar, her finely drawn tattoos shimmering in the flames of the temple's torches.

Without hesitation, she mounted me, her weight against my thighs sending waves of pleasure through my body. But even as she stroked my manhood and directed it into the inviting heat between her legs, there was something clinical about her actions. Her lips never touched my own; there was no foreplay or build-up. She simply guided me inside her and rocked back and forth, her features furrowed in concentration as she rode me.

Our coupling was clearly incidental to some higher goal. What had she said? *Accept the power I'm about to gift you.*

As we built toward a climax, I saw her tattoos deepen in color, the patterns shifting and swirling, changing like ink blots on an elaborate Rorschach test, almost like they were alive...

She began breathing faster, crashing down onto me again and again. I wanted to touch her. I ached to thrust upwards, to grab her hips, anything. But I was helpless, a spectator in this ritual. My body tightened even as her gasping breaths became a single, drawn-out cry.

We both came in a paroxysm of pain and pleasure. A strange heat engulfed my entire being, and Octurna's tattoos leapt from her skin to mine, forming new patterns and shapes all over my naked body. I screamed in exquisite agony as the living brands sank into my flesh.

The last thing I saw was Octurna's beautiful face looking down at me, her eyes coolly calculating and determined, so unlike anyone I had ever encountered in my life.

And then I mercifully passed out.

# 4

Awareness returned in a murky haze. My eyes snapped open, and for a disoriented beat, I didn't know where I was. One quick glance at my nude, newly tattooed body splayed out on the stone altar brought it all back.

My breath came in sharp bursts as memories flooded my mind with a vengeance. With them came the gnawing sense of loss. My team, my family, was gone! I shook all over as I relived each of their deaths. I wished I could have pretended that the last few hours had been nothing but a bad dream, but my surreal surroundings told me otherwise—and so did my transformed skin. I stared at the map of tattoos that now covered my body like ley lines, both horrified and fascinated by the web-like tribal patterns etched into the surface of my body. What had that woman done to me?

My chest tightened with panic. I had to stay in control. Keep a clear head.

I drew on the meditation techniques, which had been part of my morning routine since my return from Iraq, and focused on the simple act of breathing. Inhale and exhale, in and out. My nerves calmed with each successive breath, and the shaking subsided.

Somewhat.

Once I felt like I was mostly back in charge, I contemplated my next move. There was no sign of the strange sorceress who had saved me, bedded me, and branded me with her tattoos. Not even the two faceless spooks were anywhere to be seen.

I was alone in the temple.

Taking another deep, rejuvenating breath, I slipped off the altar. As I took my first tentative step, power surged through my body. I felt stronger than ever—fantastic, in fact. Energized as If I had been mainlining Starbucks Americanos and Red Bulls. My heart pounded steadily in my chest with the force of a sledgehammer. I was ready to take part in an Iron Man triathlon and walk away with a medal.

Was this a side effect of the tattoos? Or the dragon blood?

On that note, did I really believe I had consumed the blood of some mythical beast? Despite everything that had happened, I couldn't quite accept that dragon blood was now coursing through my veins. Wired and determined to get some answers to the many questions haunting me, I began to explore.

Again I marveled at the sheer size of the temple. The sprawling chamber appeared bigger from within than from without, composed of impenetrable shadow. I still didn't grasp how the small chapel I had fled into could house such a gigantic structure.

I shook my head, knowing that figuring out this crazy stuff was way past my pay grade. Considering the insane shit I'd recently experienced, it was almost funny that the scope of this place was the one detail I continued to obsess about. I had seen good men transformed into homicidal maniacs, battled a demon, and witnessed a woman heal fatal injuries with her bare hands. Not to mention the freaky, tattoo-transferring sex. Either there was more to reality than I ever suspected, or I was experiencing the most vivid fever dream ever.

To be honest, the idea of waking up in some padded cell, my system full of meds and my body constrained by a straightjacket, held some appeal. At least it would have meant the world wasn't going batshit crazy.

I was still contemplating my next move when I spotted a pile of black clothes near the altar. I had not been looking forward to exploring this drafty medieval fortress while bare-ass naked. I'm no prude, but who knew what other nasty surprises were lurking in the shadows. Facing a monster in the dark with my junk hanging out didn't sound like a good time.

I inspected the clothes. Black pants, black T-shirt, a Kevlar vest inscribed with runes and glyphs, and a leather trench coat sporting similar strange symbols, had all been neatly laid out next to a pair of badass motorcycle boots. The outfit recalled the uniform I wore in SWAT but with more of a goth flair—the Road Warrior as reimagined by Aleister Crowley.

I shrugged and got dressed. As I slipped into the black combat suit, I realized the clothes fit me like a glove almost as if the fabric had been tailored to my precise measurements. How had Octurna managed to have clothes in my exact size lying around? The answer was simple if I accepted one crazy idea—magic was real.

As I moved away from the altar, I wondered if this might be another test. Was the sorceress and her two faceless servants watching me right now, observing what I would do next? I was in no mood to play games. But I was also impatient and unwilling to sit around and twiddle my thumbs while I waited for the lady of the house—sorry, *the castle*—to grace me with her presence.

No, I needed to get out of this dungeon. Or at least get some more answers.

Mind made up, I followed the line of flickering torches which extended down the length of the temple. The shadows seemed alive with movement. Again, I felt like I had gone back in time—this was some medieval fantasy fortress straight out of *Castlevania*.

The place sure could have used a woman's touch, which was ironic considering who called it home. But the sorceress who had saved my life wasn't like any female I'd ever run into before. Who was Octurna, really? Hell, let me rephrase that question—*what* was she? A witch, or something far worse? She claimed to be human, but I wasn't convinced.

And I had slept with that creature. Well, sort of. I didn't know how to describe what had happened between us. I'd had intercourse with the hottest woman I'd ever seen and experienced the most mind-blowing yet painful orgasm of my life. Maybe I had died and gone to Hell after all.

It must have taken me ten minutes before I reached the end of the temple and arrived at a triangular wooden door. The unusual geometric shape added another surreal layer to this place, heightening the feeling that I was trapped in a dream.

I hesitated only for a beat before passing through the doorway.

The next chamber was half-moon shaped, the ceiling lower. The longer curved wall contained thousands of books lined up on shelves. The other wall was a giant stained-glass window. Waves of light emanated from the multi-colored window and painted the chamber with blue, red, and green strokes. As I drew closer, I realized the colored glass consisted of numerous smaller windows, each one depicting a unique design or a scene from some story I didn't recognize. This place couldn't seem to make up its mind—was it a church, a fortress, a castle, or something else entirely?

Navigating the chamber, I passed rows upon rows of empty display stands. It felt like I had stepped into a museum where the collection had been stolen. Only three of the stands held objects, which shone in the stained-glass windows' surreal light. The largest looked like a dinosaur skull, both reptilian and demonic in appearance, with a pair of curved horns sprouting from its bleached forehead. The monster skull would have been at home on any self-respecting heavy metal album cover.

I thought of the red liquid Octurna had poured into my mouth earlier. *Dragon Blood*. Was I looking at the skull of one of those mythical beasts?

Two other stands flanked the main one and held smaller but equally inhuman skulls. One was long and pointy with sharp, extended incisors designed to rend the flesh of its prey. The other appeared more human—except for the fangs.

"What have I gotten myself into?" I wondered out loud.

"I've been asking that same question."

I whirled, startled by the sorceress' sudden appearance. Octurna had snuck up behind me like a ninja. Shit, my situational awareness was generally off the charts. No one got the drop on me.

I stared at Octurna, waves of multi-colored light washing over her alabaster features. She freaked me out, but God was she beautiful.

"You make it a habit of creeping up on your guests?" I said for lack of a better comeback.

"I don't get too many visitors."

*No shit. I wonder why.*

"I apologize," Octurna said. "My social graces might be a little... rusty. I haven't seen another living person in over a century."

Talk about a conversation stopper. I pondered Octurna's words for a moment.

"You're over a hundred years old?" I said dumbly.

Octurna nodded, no trace of humor in her expression.

I shook my head. "What's next? You're going to tell me that you're a vampire?"

Octurna narrowed her eyes in irritation at my flippant comment. "Please, don't insult me. The Shadow Cabal created vampires."

Damn, there were way too many things wrong with that sentence.

"So vampires exist?" I asked, my voice a raspy whisper.

"Nightmares are real. I thought you'd figured out that much by now."

I shrugged. I guess I can be a slow learner.

Almost as if she'd read my mind, she said, "You must unlearn everything you thought you knew about the world, Jason."

"I'm beginning to figure that out."

"Good. It will make the next part a lot easier."

I was almost afraid of what she meant. Instead, I asked, "So are you like immortal or something?"

The sorceress shook her head. "Far from it. But the magic inside the fortress slows down the human aging process. We are beyond space and time in this place."

I was still trying to wrap my head around Octurna's latest revelation when another thought occurred to me.

"If you haven't seen a living soul in a century, then I'm the first guy you've..."

I broke off, feeling like some foolish teenager.

Octurna's expression turned business-like. "Don't read too much into what transpired between us. It was the only way I could transfer some of my magic and link my powers to you."

I cocked an eyebrow. "Are you serious?"

I felt tempted to reach out for Octurna. What would her lips feel like? They looked soft. Despite the craziness of the situation, my attraction hadn't waned. I weirdly wanted her more now than ever.

But the warning in her gaze was implicit—*don't touch me.*

"We aren't lovers, Jason, and I'm not looking for any sort of intimacy."

I stared hard at Octurna. Was she serious or trying to convince herself of her own words?

"What happened earlier was part of a ritual. A means to an end. Do you understand?"

I didn't. Not really. Then again, nothing much was making sense around here. But I could accept when a girl wasn't interested, and Octurna had cooled considerably. I backed off and did my best to change the subject.

"So these tattoos…"

"They're conduits for the magic I've shared with you."

"What are you saying? I can cast spells now?"

"Something like that. You'll need the proper training, but yes, you now can tap into the craft."

*The craft?* What was this, a goth teenager's fantasy? I felt myself growing frustrated, and it had nothing to do with being shot down by a beautiful and mysterious woman.

"Listen, lady, don't get me wrong. I'm grateful you saved my life, but I need some answers. You said you wanted me to be your knight or slayer or whatever? To fight some kind of war against monsters and magic?"

"The Midnight War. The battle between light and dark, science and magic, order and chaos, mankind and demonkind." Octurna's voice hummed with emotion while I struggled to follow her.

"Okaaay." I shook my head. This whole thing was just getting crazier by the minute. "I'm sorry, but you're losing me here."

"A short history lesson might be in order. I forget how little *regular people* know about the real world."

*You mean ordinary people who don't live in castles and whose ideas of hot first date don't include bathing in blood and having sex on stone altars*, I thought.

"I live in the real world," I said tightly. "I fought two wars in the real world."

Octurna's penetrating gaze bored into me. "I understand that all of this can be a bit overwhelming. But you've been lied to all your life, Jason. There is much more to reality than you could have ever imagined."

I could feel the muscles in my face working, and I balled my hands into fists.

"Let me show you," Octurna said.

With that, the room spun around me, and I was transported into a large cavern. A bonfire produced leaping shadows against the rough, glistening cave walls. A scraggly haired primitive man faced the flames and gesticulated wildly with his hands, his thick lips forming words in some guttural tongue. With a hiss, the fire jumped into his fingers and engulfed his whole form, imbuing him with an inner light without burning his flesh.

"Magic has been with us since the beginning, Jason. It

has always been part of the human story. It could produce wonders..."

Images of the pyramids and Mayan temples replaced the cave scenery. I felt like I had stepped into a virtual reality program where I was watching highly detailed, fully immersive 3-D holograms of the past.

"And nightmares."

My surroundings morphed again. The change was so abrupt that it triggered a wave of vertigo, and I nearly lost my balance as a brand-new landscape erased the pyramids. Nausea bubbled up my throat, and it required a great act of will to maintain my equilibrium. I now found myself in a dark, fog-enshrouded forest straight out of some fairy tale. A piercing shriek cut through the night, and I whirled.

Directly up ahead, an armored knight sat astride his horse, sword up as he confronted the darkness. Another shriek reverberated through the forest, and a bat-like humanoid monster erupted from the night. The creature dodged the knight's sword in midair and tore the doomed hero off his mount in one violent swoop. Mercifully, the giant wings hid what happened next to the writhing knight in its cruel talons. The man's blood-curdling screams drowned out the sounds of rending flesh and told their own terrifying story.

A howling sound behind me turned my blood into ice, and I pivoted on my heels. A giant wolf—no, a *werewolf*, I realized—exploded from a copse of gnarly trees and leapt at me. Fur dark as night, eyes shining with fierce intelligence. And those eyes were locked on me. Somehow, I had ceased to be a mere observer and was now part of the action. Great! Before I could shield my face from the werewolf's surprise attack, the forest rippled and warped, and I was back in Octurna's fortress.

I exhaled sharply, wiping a film of perspiration from my forehead.

Octurna's lips curled with a hint of a smile. Was she amused by my suffering?

"It would take centuries before we mastered the arcane arts," she explained. "Once we did, the magic began to flow freely through our world. Some practitioners used it to create miracles and wonders. Others allowed it to corrupt them. The worst of the lot conjured demons with their newfound powers and mixed the blood of beasts with the lifeforce of devils."

I could still taste bile in my mouth. I wanted to spit on the floor, but I didn't think the sorceress would appreciate it.

"Could you repeat that, please," I asked. "In English."

Octurna cocked an eyebrow in irritation, her patience running dry. "Mankind created the monsters of myths and legends," she said as if it were the most normal thing in the world.

Teaching wasn't the sorceress' strong suit. Hey, I didn't

even blame her. I wasn't exactly a model student. Never had been. Part of me was still in denial about all this craziness. I didn't want any of it to be true. Dammit, I wanted reality to go back to normal.

"Okay, monsters are real," I said reluctantly, still not believing it.

"The practitioners of magic knew the danger their power represented to the world, and so the Cabal was formed."

"The Cabal? Is that like the Church of Scientology?"

Octurna smiled thinly. She clearly wasn't amused. "A magical society made up by the Lords of Light, enlightened souls who had mastered the mystical arts, all of them dedicated to using their abilities as a force of good. And to ensure no one would dare break the Cabal's covenants, an order of combat magicians known as the Guardians was formed. The Guardians were entrusted with the responsibility of policing the black arts."

With each successive revelation, it all sounded more and more ludicrous. *Lords of Light? Guardians?*

Octurna's features darkened as she proceeded with her twisted history lesson. Even when I wanted to shake my head at her words, I couldn't stop looking at her. She exerted a magnetic pull on me, and the memories of our intense coupling sent a shot of heat straight to my groin.

*Hey! Snap out of it, buddy, and pay attention!*

Either unaware of the effect she was having on me or

unwilling to acknowledge it, Octurna continued her story. "Things took a dark turn a hundred years ago. Ruthless and reckless magicians arose with horrifying plans for humanity. The seven Dark Masters, as they would become known, decided to seize control of the Cabal. There was a terrible magical war. And unlike in the myths and stories, the good guys did not win. The Lords of Light were slaughtered, the Guardians hunted down. The seven Dark Masters gained control of the Cabal, and it became the Shadow Cabal. Magic would remain in our world, but the followers of the black arts would control its use and rule a new world of darkness and monsters."

I studied her face. "How do you fit into this crazy story?"

Sadness filled Octurna's expression as she spoke. "I was one of the Guardians. The only one to survive the Midnight War."

I stare at Octurna, seeing her in a new light. She too appeared to be a survivor. "How did you escape?" I asked.

"While my fellow Guardians were slaughtered like cattle, I used my last reserves of power to escape Earth and construct this fortress." Octurna swept a hand to indicate our strange surroundings.

"And where is this lovely castle?"

"The Sanctuary is a fortress outside of time and space, a place between dimensions capable of materializing anywhere on Earth. It's beyond the reach of the Shadow Cabal and its agents of chaos."

I thought about it for a moment. "So you've been hiding in this magical castle of yours for a hundred years?"

Her eyes flickered with sudden irritation. "Not hiding. Surviving. The Shadow Cabal put a death spell on me. To set foot in the real world would kill me within seconds. I would perish before I could draw my first breath. Believe me, there is nothing that I miss more than the sun shining down on my face or to breathe fresh air."

Sadness fell over the sorceress's perfect face like a veil.

At least that explained Octurna's ghostly pallor. I usually preferred ladies with a healthy tan, but her pale skin didn't detract from her attractiveness. It merely added to the otherworldly quality of her beauty.

I went over the details of her story in my mind, trying to think about it like a Marine instead of a terrified man out of his depth. "So this Shadow Cabal believes you're dead?"

Octurna nodded grimly. "Yes. They think all the Guardians have perished."

"But you're trapped here?"

"That's correct, Jason. It is both a fortress and a prison."

I pondered this for a moment. I would have gone nuts being stuck here with no one to keep me company. Almost as if Octurna had read my thoughts, she said, "Many would have succumbed to madness. But I had my hatred.

My desire for vengeance. And the knowledge that I might be humanity's last hope. I couldn't succumb to my personal demons when real ones threatened the world. I owed my masters that much. And thankfully my two constructs offered me the illusion of human company."

On cue, the two faceless beings I had met earlier materialized from the darkness. I took a quick step back. Had they been hiding in the shadows all along? So much for believing that we were alone. I eyed their mannequin faces, a shiver running up my spine. I couldn't imagine spending a day, much less a century, with those creepy creatures.

"I think I'd rather be alone," I said, suppressing a shudder.

Almost as if to prove the foolishness of my thoughts, the featureless visages shimmered and rippled. Suddenly I was looking at two gorgeous women, one a fair-skinned redhead with rosy cheeks, the other an exotic brunette.

"My constructs can be whatever you want them to be," Octurna said with the ghost of a smile.

The faces changed again, turning into male models straight out of some CW show.

"What are they?"

"Some cultures call them golems, artificial beings powered by magic. There is nothing to fear from them. They are manifestations of my will and loyal to me."

I didn't draw much reassurance from those words. I

was still trying to figure out how I felt about this sorceress, much less her two magical companions. Another thought occurred to me.

"If you've been trapped in here all this time, how did you know about me? Somehow I doubt Castle Grayskull comes equipped with a police scanner."

Octurna tilted her head toward the giant stained-glass window. "Magic," she said simply.

# 5

Octurna took a seat on the rough-hewn throne that faced the stained-glass windows. The high-backed chair was made of black stone and radiated immense power, immediately commanding respect.

The sorceress gestured at me to study the windows. I was curious, so I went along with it. As the distance shrank between me and the colorful glass, more details jumped into view. The images didn't tell some biblical story, as I had first believed. What I had initially thought to be a vast mosaic of church windows, I now realized was something far more elaborate.

As I peered at the sparkling, intricate glass tapestry, the images and figures gained detail and crispness. The glass shimmered for a beat and then morphed into images of real, moving people. For a second, I felt like I was facing a bank of CCTV monitors. But this wasn't some video feed. Each pane of stained glass had become its own window to reality.

"The magic of my windows has allowed me to follow mankind's progress, to witness our glorious triumphs and crushing defeats. But mostly the windows offer me glimpses of the dark work of the Shadow Cabal and its agents of chaos."

Octurna's words seemed far away. My attention was riveted to the human dramas playing out before me. I witnessed scenes from all across the globe, saw places I was familiar with from my days in the Marines. Iraq, Afghanistan, the Sudan. Global hotspots where misery and despair reigned supreme. Famous cities such as London, New York, Tokyo, Paris were represented too, where the smaller but equally horrific tragedies played out. I watched a group of rough kids beating up a hapless retiree for a couple of bucks; a despairing tweaker snorting meth; a security guard being gunned down by a robber in a ski mask.

After a few minutes, I became aware that Octurna had risen from her throne to join me.

"Here I've stood for the last hundred years, cursed to witness a multitude of horrors, a never-ending parade of crimes against humanity," she said. "War, famine, natural disasters, man's cruelty in all its forms. The handiwork of the Shadow Cabal."

I shot her a disturbed look. As a former Marine, one thought in particular weighed heavily on my mind.

"Are you saying the cabal is responsible for all the wars we fight?"

"Not all, but most. The Shadow Cabal keeps pushing our species toward the darkness, toward the brink. They find ways of tapping into the blackness of our souls, of using our weaknesses against us. You saw what one of their ranks did with your team. Imagine the power they wield over those with evil in their hearts. Have you wondered why the world has become such a dark place lately?"

She leaned closer and whispered, "The Shadow Cabal is winning, and humanity is losing."

My hands balled into fists. I wanted to look away from the windows. Hell, part of me wanted nothing more than to smash them to pieces. I felt helpless and enraged, desperate to step in and right the injustices but unable to do something. No wonder Octurna was a little off. I've met my fair share of cops who had succumbed to the stress of being confronted on a daily basis with the worst humanity has to offer. And this was far worse. If the police felt overwhelmed in the face of human misery, imagine being stuck here in this castle, helpless to interfere in the world's many tragedies.

My voice softened. "How have you kept going for all this time?"

She gave me a small, strained smile. "I had a mission. A

purpose. As these moments of darkness unfolded, I was looking for a champion. A hero. A man who could become my soldier in the war against the forces of darkness. I was looking for you, Jason Night."

I turned to the windows again, but I wasn't seeing them. I was reliving the nightmare at the cursed apartment building as my team slaughtered each other.

"That's how you found me," I realized. "You saw me in one of your windows. You watched while that...that *thing* killed my men."

Octurna nodded. "Yes."

In one of the stained-glass windows, a familiar scene started to unfold. I saw myself being chased by the murderous horde in the alley. Saw them tearing my vest off and stabbing me again and again. Apparently, the magic of the windows not only allowed Octurna to catch glimpses of the outside world, but she was also able to replay specific moments. Like a DVR for the universe. I shook my head, suddenly very tired.

"Why did you interfere? Why save me?"

"I already gave you the answer."

Octurna was right. She had told me she needed a knight. A slayer. Someone who could go travel between her sanctuary fortress and the real world and fight a one-man war against the darkness. She needed a Marine.

"Why me? You must've come across hundreds, maybe thousands of candidates."

Octurna's grave features flickered with amusement. "Who said you were my first choice?"

This gave me pause. Then a smile curled her luscious lips, and I knew Octurna was messing with me.

The windows lit up with new images. Glimpses of soldiers caught in the midst of combat. They wore uniforms of all colors and nations, busy fighting wars across space and time. I recognized the uniforms from various conflicts. From WW I and WW II to modern-day military conflicts. And it wasn't just Americans. All nations and countries were represented. Octurna's recruiting process seemed to extend beyond the military, too. There were cops and firefighters and other everyday heroes of all stripes. Men and women who selflessly put their lives on the line to make the world a better place. All of them heroes.

And then there was me. The lucky guy who won the lottery. Or had I pulled the short straw?

"You impressed me, Jason. Only the strongest of men can resist a succubus. I saw how bravely you fought the demon, armed with your crude, ineffective weapons. How you refused to give up when faced with overwhelming odds. But mostly, I saw how much you cared for the people under your command, the people you tried to save. You have the spirit of a warrior and the heart of a knight."

I considered this. I had just done what I thought was

right. I didn't think it was a big deal, to be honest. "Thanks, I guess. Much good it did saving anyone."

"Defeat is part of the battle. As a Marine, you know this all too well."

Unfortunately, I did. I had lost way too many friends over the years. Didn't mean I had to like it.

"My magical abilities are limited, Jason. I'm a shadow of my former self. I can maintain this place and catch glimpses of the horrors threatening humanity, but that's about it."

"Yet you shared some of your power with me. And I still don't understand what that means, exactly."

"You will. Soon enough."

"Seriously, though, I can't be the only guy you tried to recruit over the last hundred years."

"You're right. Some I failed to save in time..."

The windows showed brave men succumbing to their injuries before Octurna could intervene.

"Others who refused to accept mankind's true history."

The windows now displayed beaten, battered souls, broken men who vehemently shook their heads, refusing to accept that monsters and magic could be real.

"You've dedicated your life to making a difference in the world. To make it a better place. I'm offering you a chance to do so again."

I shook my head, overwhelmed. "I'm a cop, not some monster hunter."

I focused on the flickering mosaic of images. They had changed again. Now I caught glimpses of a myriad of inhuman beasts. Creatures that belonged in Hollywood movies, not the real world. As the monsters assaulted their victims, anger surged inside of me. I couldn't look away from the carnage. This was a new enemy for me—a very different enemy. I had faced terrorists, religious zealots, and criminals of all stripes over the years. But they all seemed like cartoon villains when compared to the horrors wreaking havoc in the stained-glass windows.

"What's the difference? The killers you battled were human, but their souls belonged to the Shadow Cabal. To the darkness. Besides, there are hundreds of thousands of cops and soldiers out there who can put an end to the next human threat. But the only ones standing between these creatures and their next victim is you and me. Mostly you."

"You make a good sales pitch, lady. I give you that."

"Does that mean you accept? Are you ready to face mankind's greatest enemy?"

I exhaled sharply and said, "I get it. These guys are bad news. But how do I hunt monsters?"

"I will teach you."

Octurna sounded almost too enthusiastic about that part.

I raked a hand across my head. "You're determined to have me go out there and fight this war for you."

"It's not my war, Jason. It's humanity's war. A fight for

the soul of our species. I've seen the Shadow Cabals' power and influence expand for a full century. Watch the news for a few minutes, and you'll see that the planet is growing darker every day. Yet I'm afraid the worst is yet to come. The Shadow Cabal won't rest until we live in a world of darkness. Each day brings us closer to that fateful day. I need someone who can stop the apocalypse before it's too late."

"And I'm the guy who will succeed where a whole magical order failed?"

"I've had nothing but time to study the enemy. I know their weaknesses. With my guidance and magic, plus your natural born skills, we have a fighting chance. And perhaps we can become an example to others who will follow our lead."

I paced back and forth, my brows furrowed in concentration as I tried to put all the pieces together so that they made sense to me. "Alright, let's say I agree to be part of this. Where do we begin?"

"The 'where' doesn't matter so much. The Shadow Cabal's forces are found all over the globe. Fortunately, my fortress can travel pretty much anywhere."

The smaller windows shimmered and warped before transforming into one giant stained-glass window that tapered in a gothic arch toward the ceiling. This new window depicted a skyline that was quite familiar to me. I was looking at the Eiffel Tower. The glass shimmered again as I stepped closer. It became a doorway opening onto the bustling French metropolis.

"One moment we can be in Paris, the next in Tokyo…"

The scene switched from daytime Paris to the bustling, glittering electronic beehive that was nighttime downtown Tokyo. Sounds of traffic drifted into the Sanctuary. I could practically smell the city outside. A few more steps, and I would find myself in Japan.

"My magic allows my fortress to blend in with the surrounding architecture. Sometimes, it might be a church or chapel, another time a house or apartment building."

I arched an eyebrow. "Won't people react to a new building popping up in their neighborhood?"

"Did you notice the chapel when your team arrived?"

I shook my head. Nothing unusual had jumped out at me, but then again, my focus had been on the mission more than the architecture.

"Only the most magically gifted people will sense that something has changed in the environment when my fortress materializes. And even those few will shrug it off the same way you did back in the alley."

I vividly recalled the moment, the brief instant of disorientation when I first took note of the chapel. Nevertheless, I had easily dismissed my surprise and rationalized it, convincing myself I had just never noticed the structure before then. I knew now that the Sanctuary's magic had been exerting its influence over my mind.

I regarded Octurna. "So this castle is your magical version of the TARDIS?"

The comment earned me a blank stare from the sorceress. Apparently Octurna didn't watch *Doctor Who*.

My attention shifted back to the crowded Japanese city, and I noticed a group of pedestrians surge past the Sanctuary's observation window. A younger girl trailing behind her distracted mother turned, eyes wide with curiosity. She shyly raised her hand and waved.

"Holy shit! She can see us, can't she?"

"As I said, only the most sensitive among them can spot my fortress. They see something, but it feels like a dream."

Tokyo vanished, and the doorway reverted back to being a bank of stained-glass windows.

"Are you ready to begin, Jason?"

I shot Octurna a long look in response. "I have a life I need to get back to."

"Is that so?" She placed a gentle hand on my shoulder. "Your parents are deceased, you have no siblings, no family. You haven't been in a serious relationship in more than two years, and your only close friends perished in that building."

Her words, so casually phrased, filled me with righteous anger. Who was she to make a judgement call about how I had lived my life? I opened my mouth to protest, but a part of me hesitated. If I thought about it, I couldn't deny what Octurna had said. My job had taken over everything else, had become my whole existence.

"People out there will miss me. Unlike my team members, I didn't leave a body behind."

She smiled again. "I wouldn't be so certain."

The stained-glass window became a giant doorway again, this time framed by an iron gate. I was now looking out at a maze of tombstones spread over a verdant green meadow.

"Go. See for yourself."

And with these words, the gate creaked open before me.

I hesitated for a beat and then jerked to attention as gunfire shredded the cemetery's tranquility. Bagpipes started to perform the familiar, soulful melody of "Amazing Grace," a tradition among funerals of cops killed in the line of duty.

"Go on," Octurna said. "You don't want to be late for your own funeral."

I glared at the sorceress and strode through the gate. My guts tightened with cold pain as I crossed the boundary between the fortress and the real world. And then the agony passed, and I felt the sun against my face, a light breeze caressing my neck.

I spun around, expecting to see the chapel from the alley but instead I now faced a medium-sized stone crypt. The gated structure blended in with the other grave markers and tombs, a natural part of the cemetery's landscape. Octurna lurked behind the crypt's wrought-iron gate and watched me with unflinching interest.

I heard a voice behind me and turned. About a hundred feet away, a burial was taking place. A priest fronted a coffin draped in an American flag, surrounded by a group of uniformed officers. Was this really my funeral?

Bile burned in my throat as I moved toward the gathering of officers. The priest was still talking, but his words failed to resonate. I needed to see the grave marker, needed to see who was being laid to rest here.

As I drew closer to the gaggle of officers, I worried what they would make of me in my long black leather trench coat and motorcycle boots. I looked like an extra from a *Matrix* reboot and would stand out like a sore thumb among these cops.

And that's when my tattoos heated up with a strange energy, and my clothes changed. The road warrior get-up morphed into a police uniform identical to the ones worn by the men and women attending the funeral. I blended in thanks to Octurna's magic.

"*Not just my magic,*" a voice said in my mind. "*Your magic, Jason.*"

I stopped in mid step, and almost lost my footing.

"*The markings on your body allow us to stay connected while you're in the outside world.*"

I took a deep breath, prayed no one else could hear

Octurna, and crossed the last few steps toward the grave. I recognized some of the officers. A few casual friends, others mere acquaintances. None of them seemed to register my presence in one way or another. To them, I was just another fellow officer joining the burial of one of their own.

Not just one of their own. Me.

Octurna hadn't been kidding. My own name was chiseled in the headstone.

But how was that possible? And didn't these people recognize me? I was standing right among them. And who the hell was in the coffin?

The sorceress's voice echoed inside my head again. *"They don't see you for who you are because your magic protects your identity."*

I moved closer to the fresh grave, and for a split second, the sunlight was just right for me to catch a vague reflection of myself in the polished marble tombstone. The face staring back at me belonged to a stranger. Overweight, bloated, sporting a thick mustache.

*What have you done to me?*

"I'm protecting you, Jason. The enemy cannot learn of your true identity. They will come after anyone you ever cared about."

*Hey, you said I had no one to leave behind!*

"Don't throw my own words back at me. *The Shadow*

*Cabal will use your past to destroy your future. Discover any weakness and exploit it."*

I glared at the headstone again, but the light quality had changed, and my reflection had vanished. Only my name stared back at me from a steel plaque, mocking. My chest burned with frustration. The rest of the funeral flashed by like in a blur, my thoughts drowned out by the melancholy tone of bagpipes. I saw men shake hands and turn away from the grave until I was the only one left standing.

*Who's in the casket?* I asked silently.

Octurna remained quiet.

*WHO IS IN THE GODDAM CASKET, OCTURNA?*

My tattoos flared, turning a fiery red. The coffin rumbled and shook. I almost jumped back as the lid burst open, revealing the corpse inside. I was staring down at myself.

I blinked. And then the face changed. I was now peering down at features that seemed distantly familiar. And then it hit me. It was the homeless guy from back in the alley behind the apartment building. The knife-wielding horde must've killed him as he was sleeping off his hangover.

And Octurna had turned him into a copy of me. A decoy.

To the world Jason Night was dead.

*"I did it to protect you, Jason."*

With a heavy heart, emotions warring inside of me, I trudged toward the waiting crypt. My clothes transformed with each step, changing back into the black combat outfit the sorceress had picked out for me.

I gritted my teeth as I passed through the creaking gate, turning my back on my old life.

*Jason Night is dead. Long live the Night Slayer.*

# 6

My heart thundered in my chest, and my muscles ached with exhaustion. Perspiration masked my face. But my eyes stayed fixed on the two golems, watching, waiting.

The first construct lashed out at me, its sword headed right for my neck. I darted aside and raised the glowing red gauntlet Octurna had armed me with. Instantly, twin blades shot from the gleaming gauntlet and blocked the incoming sword.

Magical forks of lightning exploded outward as the two charged weapons made contact.

Slightly blinded by the violent light display, I cursed under my breath and staggered backward. Luckily, the construct didn't fare much better. It recoiled, lowering its sword for a moment.

I sucked in a sharp lungful of air, the blades sprouting from my gauntlet raised like twin swords.

And why was I fighting for my life against these two faceless golems?

Let's just say Octurna was whipping me into monster hunting shape. As soon as I had returned from my own funeral, my training had begun. Grueling sparring sessions, which went on for hours, defined both my days and nights at the Sanctuary. The sorceress claimed she was preparing me mentally and physically for the many battles that lay ahead. To be honest, I was chomping at the bit to return to the real world and hunt down the succubus who had ravaged my team, but Octurna had urged me to be patient. She assured me I would get my shot at vengeance—when the time was right.

In other words, I wasn't allowed outside until Octurna thought I was ready to kick some demon ass.

Considering my military and SWAT background, I was no slouch. I was used to waving a gun around in my everyday life—responsibly, of course. But still, there was "a lot of room for improvement." That's a direct quote by the way. Octurna was always watching me, testing me. And thus far, I had failed to meet her exacting standards.

Fighting demons required a new approach, much different than police work. For one, the weapons were vastly different. Besides my magical gauntlet and a formidable arsenal of firearms loaded with silver and otherwise magically enhanced bullets, I was also learning about using magic and tapping into my dragon blood-enhanced physical abilities. I was faster, stronger, my senses sharper.

And talking about those heightened senses...

I picked up the soft rustle of the second construct's robe and spun, lightning fast. Without hesitation, I snapped a silver dagger from the bandolier strapped around my chest and flung it at my attacker. The golem's sword shot out and parried the knife aside in mid-flight.

Damn, these constructs were giving me a run for my money. I still didn't quite know how these magical beings functioned. Were they conscious entities with their own thoughts and feelings, or just puppets under the command of the sorceress? How did they process reality without visible senses?

The answer was simple: magic.

"You must move faster! Strike harder. Show no mercy."

I clenched my jaw, my irritation bubbling over. Octurna was enjoying this sparring session a bit too much. She stood in the arena's stone bleachers like some spoiled Roman empress, her regal features untouched by the many aches and pains of prolonged hand-to-hand combat. She regarded me haughtily. She was a spectator, a coach, and a critic all rolled into one hauntingly beautiful package. And she was seemingly hellbent on pushing me past my limits.

"That's your mistake, Jason. Don't set boundaries for yourself."

I shook my head. I would never get used to the sorceress poking around my mind like that.

"Knowing your limits is what keeps you alive," I growled. "And get the hell out of my head! A man deserves a little privacy."

"I thought there was no privacy in this new age of technology."

I shot a glare at Octurna, and she stayed quiet. I returned my attention to the construct wheeling toward me, determined to strike me down with its sword.

This time I anticipated the move, and the double blades of my gauntlet blocked the sword while my other hand drew one of my silver daggers and drove it into the golem's chest. The knife sliced through the creature's black robe and found the rock-solid skin underneath.

I'd already learned that throwing a punch at one of these creatures was like starting a fight with a wall. But the magical properties of silver could breach their rocklike hide, and I felt the knife sinking in.

The golem stumbled backward, dropped its weapon. Cracks formed over the surface of the faceless construct, and it shattered into a hundred pieces, the robe collapsing on top of the crumbling body.

I loomed over the downed golem, the victor for this round. Even though the construct was a pile of rubble at the moment, it would be as good as new as soon as the sorceress flicked her wrist. The same held true for yours truly if I should get badly hurt during a sparring session. I had been stabbed, gutted, and even beheaded over the course of these matches, only to be restored at the end of each fight. Somehow the arena's magic regenerated the combatants once the fight was over. It was like being part of a super-realistic video game.

Octurna was less impressed with my moves. She clapped her hands in mock applause. "Fool, don't let a short-term victory make you lose sight of the larger battle. Don't ever let your guard down until you've destroyed your enemy."

I pivoted, knowing full well that the first attack had meant to distract me and allow the second construct to sneak up on me. I drew a fiery circle of crackling energy into the air with my left hand. I could feel the complex networks of tattoos on my body igniting with incredible power as I tapped into Octurna's magic. The symbols were the conduit, the source of my new skills, but I was still learning how to use the magic.

The world turned crimson. And then an oval shield of pulsating energy exploded into existence around me. I snarled savagely as the golem's sword bounced off the magical force field.

"That's it, Jason," Octurna called from the bleachers. "Use your magic, show me what you've learned."

*I learned you can be one hell of a pain in the ass.*

I wisely didn't verbalize that thought—though much good it would do me with Octurna poking around my head whenever she seemed to feel like it.

The shield shimmered and blinked out of existence.

The construct shook off the effects and came in for another attack. This time I drew a triangle into the air, and a blast of spectral green energy shot out at the relentless golem. It sent the creature flying across the stone arena and crashing into the circular wall that separated the combatants from the overhead bleachers.

"About high time you mastered the first two spells I taught you."

This was Octurna's idea of a compliment.

My spellcasting abilities were still in their infancy as Octurna loved to remind me. Two weeks of non-stop training had allowed me to get the hang of the *Shield* and *Fireball* spells. A few days earlier, Octurna had introduced a *Teleportation* spell to my repertoire. So far I had managed only twice to transport smaller objects through space for a couple of feet and more work remained before I would master this latest trick.

While I was adding combat magic to my arsenal, I was also gaining a deeper understanding of the rules governing my new skills. My spells were fueled by Octurna's magical power source which meant that my powers were far from being unlimited. On average I could only cast two to three spells over a 24-hour period but mileage might vary depending on the exact nature of the magic trick.

The important takeaway was that I wouldn't be able to win any battles using only my mystical skills. The spells were an excellent addition to my arsenal and would serve me well in a pinch, but for the most part I would have to rely on my weapons and reflexes. Fortunately, the dragon blood had done wonders for my strength and reaction speed.

"Finish your enemy," Octurna urged me.

My eyes blazed as I zeroed in on the downed construct, gauntlet ready to plunge into the thing's throat. But the golem had no qualms with playing dirty.

As I drew closer, the creature's mannequin face morphed into that of a terrified woman. Blonde hair spilled from the hood of her robe, her big eyes stained with tears. Big softie that I am, I hesitated for a moment. That's all it took for the golem to spring back to its feet and lunge at me, sword eager to pierce my foolish heart. And this time I wouldn't be able to conjure a force field around me.

Reacting on pure instinct, I jumped. The dragon blood coursing through my body catapulted me upwards. The sword-wielding golem, still wearing the face of a murderous pin-up girl, passed six feet underneath me, her blade slicing thin air where my neck had been seconds earlier.

I spun around in mid-air and drove my gauntlet into the golem with savage ferocity as I descended. The second construct went down in a heaving mess. Blood burst from those lovely features, and I turned away, shaken by the sight of the dying woman. Call me old-fashioned, but I don't make it a habit of engaging the opposite sex in gladiatorial matches to the death.

"You're a real gentleman, Jason. How sweet. That kind of weakness will get you killed out there."

"Hey, I'm not a monster!" I protested.

"Then how do you expect to defeat monsters? Do you fight with what's between your legs or what's in your hands? You hesitated as soon as you saw a pretty face."

I glared at Octurna, upset that she was right. The golem's transformation had made me pause. Fuck, I'm only human, I thought.

"And then you'll die like a human."

Octurna leapt at me from the arena's bleachers. Her red robe billowed around her as she soared toward me, her eyes blazing.

Stunned, I backed off. The sorceress had never joined the battle before, and it took me by surprise.

"You think the Shadow Cabal will fight fair?" she hissed. "You think that succubus will play by the rules when you face her again?" There was a flash of sizzling energy and the downed golems' swords materialized in both of Octurna's hands.

She rushed at me, eyes gleaming with lethal intensity. I reflexively brought up my gauntlet. The twin blades exploded through the pale skin of her swanlike neck in a spray of red. Shock rippled through me as the life left those mesmerizing emerald eyes, her gaze going blank. What had I done?

I dropped my arm, and Octurna's gored form slipped off the crimson blades. I gently caught the sorceresses' body and lowered her to the ground, my hand cradling her head.

A shiver ran up my spine, and my chest tightened. Dammit, Octurna had pretty much thrown herself into my blades...

And that's when mocking laughter rang out around me. It echoed through the arena.

I looked up from the defeated witch and found myself surrounded by five robed figures who all looked like Octurna.

My initial shock turned to rage. The sorceress was messing with my head again. Another illusion, another game.

"Not games, my dear knight. Tests. What sort of monster do you take me for? I'm not going to send a child to do a man's job."

My lips pressed into a determined line as I whipped out two more daggers and hurled them at Octurna's taunting mirror images. The knives cut through the air and struck two of the clones in their hearts.

They collapsed as I sprang to my feet, the blades on my gauntlet thirsty for more blood. Steel flashed, and I hacked a violent path through the circle of magical duplicates. I had grown tired of the sorceress' manipulative games, her constant air of superiority. I was tired of this place, of the hours of training, of being trapped in a nightmare from which I couldn't wake.

I wanted to return to my world, wanted to get the hell out of this haunted castle where you never knew what was real and what was just another magic trick.

I wanted my old life back, for fucks sake.

I cut the sorceress down again and again, blocking her vicious attacks, like an unstoppable machine that wouldn't rest until my blades found an opening. Who knows how long the fight raged in the arena? All I remember is growing still when the last copy collapsed. I was surrounded by the broken forms of the sorceress, the air thick with blood and perspiration, the double knives of my gauntlet slick with gore.

"Are you happy now?" I growled. My voice sounded barely human to me, more beast than man. "Am I what you want me to be?"

"It's not about what I want you to be," a voice answered. I spun around, and Octurna was back in the bleachers, unharmed. The superior attitude was gone, replaced with a somber expression. Did I detect a hint of sadness in her perfect features, a chink in her icy armor? "This is what you have to become if you want to survive what lays ahead."

A rumbling sound rang through the arena as the steel door swung open. The sparring session was over. Time to go back to my quarters.

"You had best get cleaned up," Octurna said as I dragged my exhausted ass to the arena's exit. "There are matters we must discuss."

I frowned. This was a new development. Usually these sessions ended with Octurna wordlessly disappearing into the shadows, leaving me to return to the room she'd assigned to me in the Sanctuary. I would retire for a few hours of sleep before the golems would drag me from bed, and the same torture would repeat itself.

It sounded like things might play out differently this time around. The thought that I might get to face a monster soon spiked my adrenaline levels and even put a bounce in my steps despite my tiredness.

I walked through the open doorway and saw the two downed golems rise from the arena floor. No traces of their terrible injuries remained. Sure would be nice if it worked like that in the real world.

Exhaustion enveloped me as I made my way down a stone hallway lit by a row of sconces and up a winding staircase. The Sanctuary felt like a cross between Castle

Grayskull and the Batcave, a multi-leveled labyrinth of hidden rooms, dim passageways and secret chambers, an area of mystery and ancient forbidden knowledge. Homey it wasn't. And I very much doubted I could last a month in this spooky place, much less a whole century.

The door to my sleeping quarters opened before I could even touch the handle. It was one of the many unnerving details that defined life in the Sanctuary.

I entered the chamber, and the door slammed shut behind me.

*I can open and close my own door, thank you very much*, I thought.

Somehow, the tattoos I now shared with Octurna allowed her to track me at all times. Privacy didn't exist in this place, and I couldn't shake the impression that some magical camera was following my every move. The sorceress wasn't letting me out of her sight, and it was driving me up the wall. I was used to having my freedom. Making matters worse, Octurna knew all my secrets while I knew none of hers. I was an open book while she remained an unsolvable puzzle.

Octurna stayed quiet on her end. Good. I was in no mood to talk, to be honest. My stomach growled as I fought back a yawn. The hours of combat had wiped me out, and I was looking forward to a hot bath, some good food, and the soft sheets of my bed. From experience I knew the moment I closed my eyes, Octurna's loyal constructs would barge into my quarters and drag me to the next test or sparring lesson. Better to enjoy the momentary reprieve from the grind while I could.

My chambers held a certain medieval charm. There were no windows, but more sconces offered generous illumination. A fur rug of some beast I couldn't—and probably wouldn't want to—identify covered the stone floor, and a queen-sized bed decked out in soft, inviting blankets waited for my exhausted muscles.

I stripped off my clothes, snatched a towel, and wiped myself down. My stomach rumbled, reminding me that I needed a snack before my bath. I must've burned thousands of calories over the course of the last few hours of non-stop sparring. I had always been in fighting shape, but now there was not even an inch of fat around my waist.

My eyes lit up excitedly when I spotted plates of food waiting for me on a nearby table. There was a bowl of fresh fruit and cheeses, a second bowl of mixed walnuts, pecans, and hazelnuts. I greedily grabbed a handful of nuts and washed them down with a flask of mineralized water. Then my attention turned to the delicious smelling chicken sitting on a silver platter. I had no idea how Octurna procured healthy, fresh food on a daily basis, not to mention who had prepared these delicacies. I didn't quite see Whole Foods making deliveries to the Sanctuary, and Octurna certainly wasn't the type to slave over a hot stove.

Then again, I had quickly learned to stop asking questions around this place, especially once I realized there would be no answers. Octurna had her way of doing things, and that was that.

My hunger somewhat satiated, I relaxed a little, and my breathing steadied. I was looking forward to washing all the blood and sweat and grime off my battered body. There was no form of entertainment in this place, no TV or internet or even books I could read. The only books were the ones downstairs in the observation chamber, and most of them were written in languages long dead and forgotten. Well, almost forgotten. Clearly, my lovely host had no problem understanding them. Even if the texts were in English, I doubted I would have been able to make heads or tails out of the knowledge contained within those pages.

I finished undressing and turned to the adjoining bathing area. Calling it a bathroom didn't quite do it justice. The first time I explored my quarters, a part of me thought I had taken a wrong turn and accidentally ended up in the infamous grotto at the Playboy mansion. An expansive jacuzzi had been carved into the rock, the water kept at the perfect temperature. More water flowed down the cave walls, springing from some unknown source. I decided to not waste any more mental energy trying to figure out how this place worked and tried to enjoy myself. Maybe the sorceress was too weak to battle dragons and super wizards, but she had enough juice left to keep her Sanctuary running in style.

The water both relaxed and invigorated my sore muscles. I dipped under and closed my eyes, doing my best to block everything out for a few blissful moments. But images from my crazy new life intruded my thoughts. And foremost among them was Octurna herself. I saw her glistening, naked body in my mind's eye, remembered the heat of our physical encounter on the altar. I hated her drill sergeant ways and how she kept me at arm's length but another part...okay, I admit, inviting her over for a dip in the hot tub had crossed my mind.

*Get your head on straight, buddy, and I'm talking about the one between your ears.*

But now that I had eaten my evening meal, another appetite was taking hold. A sound near the door drew my attention. I let out a surprised gasp when I realized I wasn't alone in the grotto anymore. Two monk-like figures peeled from the shadows, their faces shrouded by their hooded robes.

Fantastic. Instead of the beautiful sorceress, her golems had decided to pay me a visit.

"Hey, guys, don't you think it's a bit too early for a rematch?" I said.

"That's up to you to decide, slayer," a rich, husky voice replied.

The robes slipped from Octurna's magical constructs,

revealing two gorgeous women. They were tall and athletic, with curves in all the right places.

"I am Nuala," the one on the left said. "And this is Zemira."

Both the beauties appeared to be multiracial, as though all of my fantasies had been blended together to create the women standing before me. Nuala had bronzed skin with vaguely Japanese features and dark hair that fell in a smooth wave down her back. Zemira had curly caramel-colored hair a shade or two lighter than her complexion and a full, pouty mouth.

"You fought well today, Jason. The sorceress wants you to have some fun," Zemira said, taking a step toward me.

Fucking a rock creature wasn't my idea of fun. But neither Nuala nor Zemira shared much in common with the faceless mannequins that snuck around this place like a couple of spooks—and that only minutes earlier had tried to kill me.

The first goddess stepped into the Jacuzzi and drifted toward me, her ample cleavage carving the water's surface. I sat there as if frozen, my body responding to the sight of these two gorgeous creatures even while my mind reeled. I tried to think of them as the faceless golems I had battled in the arena but couldn't.

"You've trained hard for the last two weeks," Zemira said. "The sorceress feels you deserve a reward."

"Uh, I'm good, thanks. I don't need a reward!"

My body seemed to have a different opinion about that.

"Why do you fight what your body craves?" Nuala purred.

Good question. To be honest, I wasn't putting up too much of a fight. Nuala pressed against my muscular frame. I automatically reached out and drew her closer, her breasts brushing against my chest. From the corner of my eye, I saw Zemira circle us and lean into me from behind, her hands running down the sore muscles of my broad back, exploring.

Screw it. A man has needs, right? I buried my face in Nuala's cleavage. The dragon blood had increased both my stamina and sexual appetite, and I felt like an uncaged lion as I claimed the two Amazons who gave themselves so willing to me. Soft lips trailed kisses over my skin, and hands caressed me everywhere at once.

But as I built up to my release, I found my mind turning to another woman. One with snow-white skin and a haughty smile.

## 7

For the first time since starting my new life at the Sanctuary, I slept like a baby. When I awoke—alone, I might add—I felt energized and refreshed. For a change, Octurna hadn't deemed it necessary to wake me in the middle of the night for more training. As much as I appreciated feeling well rested, I was suspicious of the sorceress' sudden generosity. Why had she sent the golems to my quarters and turned them into sex- crazed Barbies?

My blissful hours spent with Octurna's magical assistants filled me with mixed emotions. I wasn't proud of myself. They weren't people, not really. But they'd seemed so real. I wished I could blame too much wine for what had gone down last night. But I guess I'd needed the release after the last few weeks of torture. Still, who or *what* did I have sex with? And the next time

I faced them in the gladiator torture chamber, I doubted I could think of Nuala and Zemira as two faceless mannequins.

I got dressed and ate an apple. As soon as I took the last delicious bite, the door of my sleeping quarters opened. Right on schedule. Did Octurna ever take her eyes off me?

Had she been watching me last night? Did she enjoy the show?

I sighed and stepped out of my room. It didn't come easy to a guy like me, but I had to accept that Octurna was in charge. At least for the moment. If this arrangement was going to work, I would have to swallow my pride and play along. Didn't mean I had to like it.

*"Don't be so dramatic, Jason. It doesn't become a warrior."*

I flinched as my tats lit up, and Octurna's seductive voice filled my mind. I wisely avoided being baited into an argument regarding what was becoming or not in a so-called warrior.

"What's on the schedule today?" I inquired. "Are we gearing up for another round in the arena?"

*"No. Today we take the fight to the Shadow Cabal. Meet me downstairs in the library."*

The sorceresses' words sent a shiver up my spine. My body tingled with a mixture of excitement and anxiety. This was it. I was finally going to get a real fight.

"So does that mean we're done with the training?"

"Far from it. I hesitate sending you into the field ill-prepared as you are, but the enemy has forced our hand."

I wasn't sure if I should feel insulted by this blunt assessment or worried.

"You know, being locked away from humanity sure has done wonders to your social skills."

*"What's your excuse, brute?"*

I shook my head and decided to drop it. It was too early, and I was in far too good of a mood to get into a verbal sparring match with my supernatural hostess. Instead, I did my best to maintain a positive attitude and an open mind as I descended the stairs.

Most of the Sanctuary remained a mysterious labyrinth to me, but after spending a few weeks here, I knew how to get from my quarters to the library. Waves of blue-red light washed over me as I joined Octurna in the circular chamber. She faced the shimmering bank of stained-glass windows, unmoving as a statue, her gorgeous features locked in an intense mask of concentration. From my vantage point, the windows still looked like painted glass. Only once I drew closer to her did the windows change, offering glimpses into the real world.

"So what's the scoop?" I struggled to keep my tone even and measured. It did not become a warrior to sound too excited, right?.

Octurna didn't turn to look at me. "I hope my constructs were to your satisfaction?"

I shrugged, not sure how to respond to that question. "I feel well rested," I said at last.

"Good. I thought you had earned a reward for your dedication."

"Thanks, I guess."

*So why didn't you swing by yourself*, I wondered.

For a beat, we stood in front of the windows in awkward silence.

"What are we looking at?" I asked.

"The dark handiwork of our first target."

I concentrated on the windows, allowing the details to come into focus. They showed multiple crime scenes. Bodies that had been discarded in city alleys, subway tunnels, and sewers. All the victims were male and looked as though their chests had been torn open. My good mood dissipated as the harsh reality of what I faced settled in.

"The succubus has been busy," Octurna said.

She pointed at two more windows, which showed medical examiners inspecting the murder victims over autopsy tables. The harsh halogen glow of the forensic lab's lights revealed all the gruesome details. I couldn't hear what the MEs were saying, but the ragged cavities in the victims' chests told their own grim story.

"She took their hearts?"

Octurna nodded. "The mark of the succubi."

"I thought she infected people the way she did back in the building, turning them into crazy zombies?"

"No, she was ravenous when she first arrived in our world. Normally, her kind is selective about their victims. They target either males or females, depending on their preferences, and then seduce them, even make them fall in love, before feasting on their crushed hearts and lovesick souls."

"Sounds like a couple of my exes."

This statement earned me a cocked eyebrow from the sorceress. She wasn't amused at my half-assed attempt at humor.

"Sounds to me like you show poor judgment in your selection of mates."

I raised an eyebrow right back at her. "Hey, you tell me."

Octurna held my gaze for a beat. Christ, a man could get lost in that hypnotic gaze. It felt like the sorceress was looking into my soul. It took all my will power to resist pulling her toward me for a kiss.

"Okay, what else have we got? What do we know about the vics?"

"Six dead so far. As you can see, none of the victims were exactly prime physical specimens." Octurna was referring to their bloated faces, bulging waists, and receding hairlines. Poor bastards. "All of them were middle-aged, unhappily married or recently divorced, and flush with cash."

I chewed this over. "Go on."

"Succubi feed on emotion. Consuming the heart is symbolic. Some of them find betrayal to be a delicacy, so she might enjoy convincing these men to love her before revealing how badly they'd been fooled."

"How does she hunt these victims?"

"All of these poor fools had plenty of disposable income. Where do men with too much money, bulging waistlines, and raging hormones go when they are feeling *lonely?*"

The way she pronounced *lonely* made me think of a very different word. I already knew the answer to Octurna's question before the palace of flashing neon filled one of the stained-glass windows. The strip club was called *Island Fantasy*, its fiery red letters impossible to miss.

"Are you telling me an interdimensional being has nothing better to do than set up shop in a titty bar?"

Octurna shrugged. "The succubus is a predator and follows its prey. Quite cunning, but still a beast driven by its baser desires and needs. Honestly, she is nothing but a lower-level demon."

A lower-level demon who had wiped out my entire team, ruined my life, killed an entire building's worth of college kids, and since then had added six more poor schmoes to its growing list of victims. I didn't want to think of the kind of chaos a full-fledged demon could cause.

"I know this is personal for you, Jason. And I believe you stand a chance against this enemy."

I gave Octurna a long look. "Thanks, I think."

"Are you ready to avenge your fallen brothers and sisters?"

I grimly eyed the dead men whose only fault had been to seek love and comfort from a beautiful woman. In a strip club. Okay, maybe they were sleazebags. But being a middle-aged horndog didn't mean you deserved to get your heart torn out of your chest.

"I'm ready."

"Are you sure? You're going up against a formidable enemy here."

"Listen, this isn't my first rodeo..."

She frowned. If I didn't know better, I'd almost mistake her expression for concern. "This war is nothing like the ones you fought on Earth."

"You've never faced the Taliban on the battlefield, have you now?"

The momentary softness in her expression crystalized into her usual hauteur. "And you've never faced a werewolf ready to tear out your throat with his bare teeth."

Touché.

"Are you trying to talk me into this crazy war or out of it? I'm ready. As ready as I'll ever be."

Octurna regarded me for a beat. Then she flashed me a satisfied smile and pointed to my right. I turned, and my gaze landed on the most badass motorcycle I'd ever seen.

This was love at first snarling engine roar. I'd ridden

since I was sixteen and owned multiple bikes over the years, but this was a set of wheels in a league of its own.

I let out a low, appreciative whistle as I advanced. The bike must've sensed my approach. The engine revved and the hog lit up with a spectral green light. Orange flames licked the tires.

"Holy Shit! Don't tell me this is a magical motorcycle?"

"Haven't you learned anything in the last month? Everything is magical here."

No kidding.

"So what can it do?"

"You'll figure it out soon. The *Nighthawk* has a few tricks up its sleeve."

*Nighthawk*? Was Octurna having a joke at my expense?

I drew closer to the bike, admiring the cycle's ferocious design and throbbing horsepower. Visually, it resembled the Triumph Rocket III, which I had been eyeing for a while. I had a feeling this bike's specs would put the Rocket to shame. I circled the roaring cycle, eying it with respect as it bucked like a wild bronco. I felt like a sixteen-year-old kid again, about to take my first set of wheels for a spin.

I was ready to conquer the world.

"You will need this," the sorceress said.

Octurna waved her hands, the air crackled and shifted around me, and the bladed gauntlet appeared around my right hand. And that was just the beginning. Octurna's magic had fully armed me. Strapped around my shoulder was my submachine gun, but with a few new mods. It looked like it a prop from some Hollywood science fiction flick, crossed with my beloved HK MP5, with some runic engravings for good measure. A weapon both familiar and fantastical. Over the course of my training sessions, I had learned that the rifle fired both silver ammo and magic-charged bullets. I also sported a 9mm handgun loaded with silver ammo.

I touched the daggers sheathed on my bandolier. Between the two spells I'd mastered, the machine pistol, the knives, the 9mm handgun and the gauntlet, I felt pretty much invincible. I'd seen enough combat to know that this feeling would wear off soon enough, but for now, I enjoyed the ride.

A thought occurred to me. "Okay, I have some serious firepower here, but what happens if I need cash or an ID?"

Octurna considered this. She opened her hand and tossed me a glittering object. I caught the gold coin, which twinkled in the multi-colored light.

"Your missions, if you should survive tonight, will take you all over the globe. The coin can become any currency as needed," Octurna explained like it was a normal, common thing.

I was still wrapping my head around this latest revelation when Octurna removed a star-shaped medallion from a necklace which she wore around her neck. It shimmered ominously as she handed it to me. I took note of the series of sigils engraved in the metal. I was still studying the jewelry when it morphed into my driver's license. Within seconds it became an FBI badge, a police badge, and then a military ID. Whoa.

"The medallion can become any form of identity you may need while carrying out your missions. You'll be able to visit crimes scenes, infiltrate government and other secure buildings. And I think that's quite enough to get started. Now go!"

Feeling like the biggest badass in the universe, I straddled the humming hog. Doubt filled my heart for a split second—I was on a collision course with fate. Could I conquer the challenges that lay ahead? Was I ready to face the demon? I was a cop, not some comic book superhero. But then I thought of the friends I'd lost to the succubus, and my face tightened with steely determination. There was no turning back. I had sworn my life to protecting the innocent. Time to see what I was made of.

To my surprise, Octurna approached and laid a gentle hand on my cheek. The tattoos covering my skin pulsed briefly at the contact.

"I will monitor your progress and remain in contact while you make your way in the outside world. You won't be alone out there, Jason Night. Godspeed"

I nodded, ignoring the sick feeling in the pit of my gut. God seemed very far away.

**8**
---

The tapestry of stained-glass shimmered and warped, light bending and twisting as a giant doorway to reality opened up before me. I was never going to get used to this. Outside the magical portal, the sun was setting over the glittering Los Angeles skyline, and I could almost taste the smog drifting into the Sanctuary's library.

To the naked eye, it looked like only a few feet separated me from the streets of LA. But in reality, I was looking out from one dimension into another. It's hard to wrap your mind around the concept. Trust me, I know.

I revved the *Nighthawk,* took a deep breath, and exploded through the interdimensional gateway. As I passed from the Sanctuary into the real world, my stomach lurched and my hairs stood up, magical energy sizzling around me. By the time I exhaled, I found myself surrounded by long-abandoned warehouses and tenement buildings. This wasn't exactly one of the popular sections of downtown Los Angeles. Still, after being stuck for three long weeks in Octurna's castle, it felt like paradise. The city lights shimmered up ahead, and I struggled to wipe the big grin off my face. The air was thick and stifling, the sounds of traffic loud, yet I was in heaven. The sounds of the city energized me after the silence of the Sanctuary. I had missed my hometown something fierce.

I stole a glance backward and couldn't entirely hide my wonder at seeing the Sanctuary transformed into a rundown hotel that blended in with the other buildings in this neglected part of the city. It made me think of the famous Chateau Marmont on Sunset, its European flair and castle-like towers sharp reminders that this was no ordinary hotel. Octurna stood in the doorway, her eyes following my departure, unable to join me unless she wanted to risk the consequences of the Cabal's death spell. She was indeed a prisoner inside her magical fortress.

Was there a longing in her eyes? A sadness in the slight downturn of her lips?

*"Under that macho veneer, you're a real poet, Jason. Now focus on the road."*

Octurna's voice inside my head shattered any sympathy I might feel for the sorceress. Even out here in the real world, our telepathic link persisted.

Almost as if to confirm this connection, the tattoos lit

up all over my body. Octurna's power raged inside me, and as long as it did, the sorceress would always be with me.

*"You make it sound so tragic, Jason."*

*Hey, I like my privacy. Now let me concentrate on the road.*

I twisted the handlebars, took a sharp turn, and shot down into an even seedier section of the city. The strip club was located right off the 101 freeway, surrounded by several blocks of a homeless tent village. The club took advantage of the relative isolation downtown offered compared to the rest of Los Angeles. Their homeless neighbors wouldn't complain about loud drunkards partying late into the night.

An icy chill pricked my back as my thoughts turned to the Shadow Cabal. If man's inhumanity toward his fellow man wasn't bad enough, now I had to worry about a crazy syndicate of mages who were hoping to turn the world into a Club Med for demons.

Hey, at least my life wasn't dull.

I shot past a fast food burger joint and started to salivate. One thing was certain—once I finished off my business with the succubus, I was going to grab myself an In-N-Out burger, the greasiest taco truck burrito I could get my hands on, and a cold IPA. There are certain things a man can't live without.

*"What's so special about this In-N-Out Burger?"* Octurna inquired.

*It only happens to be the best damn burger on the planet.*

*Talk about real magic. If you stay out of my head, I might get you one on the way back.*

With a grin on my face, I cranked the engine, excited by the prospects of a juicy burger.

"*I never witnessed a warrior walking into battle with such a favorable disposition, Jason. Are you taking this seriously?*"

*Hey, I'm having a moment here. Please don't ruin it.*

"*I am...legitimately worried about your chance of survival. You had best accept the gravity of the upcoming battle if you hope to walk away from it in one piece.*"

*Don't sweat it, Octurna. I got this.*

I doubted the sorceress shared my confidence, but at least my words stopped her incessant whisperings in my head.

As I blasted down the next few blocks, my elated mood evaporated. Grim thoughts settled into my mind. The initial excitement of being back in the world was wearing off, and the reality of what I was up against dawned on me. I was about to confront a creature that had managed to take out a full SWAT team. This monster had almost killed me once before. I would have died if Octurna hadn't stepped in. At least I came prepared for my rematch. I was armed to the teeth with a badass magical arsenal and had a better sense of the nightmarish shit storm I was about to enter.

I was ready for this fight. Needed it. Or at least that's what I was telling myself. The closer I got to the strip club, the more the waves of adrenaline ebbed off and fear rose inside of me.

Fear was good, I told myself. Fear kept your guard up. Fear kept you alive. Thank God for my years in the Marines. That training, paired with what I'd learned in Octurna's fortress, would see me through this.

I hoped.

Dread in my heart, I stared at the ugly, square building that would have smoothly blended in with the other abandoned warehouses except for the flashing neon signs on its roof. *Island Fantasy* was no island, and I was pretty sure the joint disappointed on the fantasy front too.

I pulled up to the structure and parked the *Nighthawk*. As I killed the engine, I wondered if the cycle would be safe in this seedy part of town. Octurna hadn't provided me with a lock or chain. The idea of some thief getting away on my magical bike didn't sit well with me.

*"Don't worry, the motorcycle is protected. Any fool dumb enough to touch it will flashback to their worst childhood memories and be reduced to a blubbering mess,"* Octurna chimed in helpfully.

With a last, lingering look, I made my way to the strip club. I'd fallen hard for my new ride. The thought that someone might try to steal her made me physically ill.

Booming music drifted from the main entrance, where a monster of a man kept his watchful eye on the clientele. I worried that I might look a tad intimidating in my Road

Warrior get-up, but as I looked down at myself, I realized I was wearing a cheap, sweat-stained suit and a Rolex that uncomfortably bit into my chubby wrist. My clothes had changed without me even noticing. I felt for the coin in my suit pocket and came up with a stack of twenties and ones. I silently wondered how Octurna knew what the going rate for a lap dance was in the twenty-first century.

I stepped up to the bouncer who regarded me with a blank, bored expression. My disguise was working. I just looked like another sucker eager to trade my hard-earned cash for a serious case of blue balls.

He waved me inside, and I entered the pleasure den.

A bored looking woman who had to be in her thirties and a few pounds too heavy for the stage eyed me with a tired, jaded expression. Ex-stripper who had made the career jump to door person—I could tell she loved her life.

I paid the cover charge and stepped into the garish flesh palace. The AC was cranked up too high, and I felt terrible for the scantily clad girls shaking their asses on stage and hustling patrons for drinks and dances or both. Two neon-lit stages rose above the tawdry red carpet. Mirrors were everywhere, making the club appear larger than it was, an effect enhanced by the low, moody lighting.

I eyed my reflection for a beat. The face staring back made me shudder. It was me but about a hundred pounds heavier. A double—correction, triple—chin, and I was pretty much bald with only grey tufts above my ears reminding the world that once upon a distant time I'd possessed a full head of hair. It was an image I wouldn't get out of my head any time soon. But man, I sure looked like the perfect mark.

*"Excellent job, Octurna,"* I thought.

*My pleasure, handsome.*

I could almost hear the sorceress laughing. I wasn't amused.

Strangely enough, even though I looked like I was one meal shy of a heart attack, my body felt the same to me. At least that meant I hadn't actually physically transformed. Octurna's magic was no joke. The big question was if this trick of smoke and mirrors would work on a demon. The sorceress seemed to believe so. I hoped she was right.

*"Have some faith in me, Jason."*

I headed for the bar and purchased a Coors Light, making sure to tip generously. I had no idea who among the dancers was the succubus. The plan was to let the creature come to me.

Beer in my grubby hand, I took a seat in one of the gaudy purple chairs surrounding the larger stage. A tiny Asian beauty hung upside down from the stripper pole, one leg wrapped around the shiny metal while the other pointed toward the dance floor. Talk about flexibility. The girl looked like she might be ready for Cirque du Soleil tryouts.

I sipped my drink and let my gaze roam the joint. How to pick out the demon from all the other dancers?

The women came in all shapes and sizes and ethnicities. A little something for everyone. But none of them particularly moved me. They couldn't hold a candle to the Amazons that had shared my bed last night.

Oh hell. Last night's adventure in the grotto suddenly made more sense. Octurna had made sure I wouldn't get distracted while on the job. Christ, the sorceress had thought of everything. Kinda scary how she did that.

That said, neither lap dances nor strip clubs were my scene. Personally, I considered them a waste of hard-earned cash I'd rather spend on a date with a real girl than on some two-minute fantasy. But I planned to buy a few dances to attract the attention of the succubus.

It's a hard gig, but someone's got to do it.

After the fifth girl collected her twenty-dollar bill, I was beginning to wonder if I might need a better plan. And then girl number six showed up, and my tattoos lit up with agony almost as if I was sporting fresh ink.

I studied the gorgeous creature in front of me. The previous dancers had been attractive enough. Girl number six undeniably was a vision. A natural beauty, nothing fake here, with a big smile and even bigger eyes. A body made for sin, a face of an angel. While my tattoos were telling me she was the succubus, the rest of me wanted to save her from a future in a place like this. Honestly, she was the last dancer in the club I would have suspected of being a demon.

Octurna's words echoed through my mind: Don't trust surface appearances. Boy, she hadn't been kidding. The succubus had altered her appearance from the femme fatale I'd first encountered with my team. Like Octurna's golems, her appearance seemed to be fluid and specific to the fantasies of her potential victims.

I guess I had a thing for the girl-next-door who needed rescuing.

The succubus flashed me a friendly, inquisitive look. "And what's your name, sugar?"

"Joe," I said, the lie rolling off my tongue.

She innocently offered me her hand. Shaking a scantily clad girl's hand in this place felt surreal. "Nice to meet you, Joe. My name is Sasha. Are you having a good time?"

I nodded my head, perhaps a tad too quickly. Her wholesome appearance was throwing me off. Octurna was wise to test me in the arena the way she had. This might prove tougher than I imagined. I was a sucker for a pretty face.

*"The succubus is manipulating you,"* Octurna said, but her voice didn't seem quite as loud in my mind as it had before.

I wanted to believe that Octurna's magic could be

wrong, wanted to give this lovely creature the benefit of the doubt.

*"Snap out of it, Jason. My magic doesn't lie. Don't let yourself be played for a fool unless you want to end up like the others. Don't be such a... man!"*

I ignored Octurna and focused on Sasha.

The wholesome-looking stripper sat down beside me, and we started to chat. Talk about a lively exchange. There were no awkward pauses, no lulls in the conversation. Somehow Sasha kept the flow going, making it seem both natural and fun, and like we'd known each other for way longer than five minutes. Even though I tried to tell myself over and over again that I was dealing with a murderous predator here, I kept finding myself getting lost in her eyes. Sasha sure could make a man feel like the center of the universe.

*"Remember what she is. What she did to your team."*

Along with Octurna's words, images of my slaughtered team flashed through my mind. Sasha's smiles suddenly seemed less genuine, her beauty less intoxicating. I clung to the images of carnage and despair. I forced myself to picture each of my dead teammates even though it hurt. I focused on the memory of the reptilian beast that hid under this skillfully crafted façade. I had resisted her charms once before. I could do it again.

*I know what you are,* I silently promised. *And tonight, I will send you back to Hell.*

Sasha still smiled and joked and flattered me at every turn, but she had stopped weaving a spell over me. Her magic was powerful, but so was the memory of my dead friends.

*Thank you, Octurna. I owe you one.*

My initial infatuation gave way to anger and then hatred. Hatred for what this creature had done to my friends. Done to me. And what it was doing to innocent people. She was a monster. And I was going to kill her or die trying in the process.

"Do you want to go to the champagne room with me?" the succubus asked.

I flashed a happy grin and nodded enthusiastically. Inside, I cringed at the thought of this monster rubbing up against me. I was already thinking of ways of luring the succubus out of the club so I could finish her.

*Be patient*, I told myself. Take a page from her playbook. Lure her into a false sense of security and control. Let her lower her guard. And then strike without mercy.

Sasha grabbed my hand, and I let her lead me to the back of the club. The envious looks of the other patrons followed us.

The back room was even chillier than the main floor of the club. I guess they didn't want anyone to get too comfortable, and the cold did have a sobering effect. I pretended to respond to Sasha's words and the sensuality of her dancing—and kept feeding her bills, creating the impression that I was another mark smitten by her. This is what the succubus wanted. She fed on emotion and need.

I looked up at her, pretending to be a man madly in love. "I've never met anyone like you, Sasha. I...I don't want to seem forward, but is there a way we could continue this in a more private setting?"

This was it. I was setting my trap. I prayed I hadn't overplayed my hand. The succubus hadn't murdered her victims in the club, so in each instance she had found a way to meet up with them elsewhere. The club was her web but not the place where this black widow finished off her prey. Confronting her here would draw attention and most likely get innocent men and women killed. The chance for collateral damage was way too high.

The succubus' eyes lit up, and a devilish smile played over her lips.

"Someone wants to be naughty tonight."

I shrugged, feigning sudden shyness, playing up the role of the middle-aged schlub who was about to do something foolish but couldn't help himself. I pulled out a roll of hundred-dollar bills. The gold coin in my suit jacket seemed to be printing money, creating new wads of cash as soon as I needed them. Man, this magic would have sure come in handy during my last Vegas trip.

Our little moment was ruined by the bouncer. He stuck his head through the door and barked, "Sasha, get your ass on stage!"

The succubus' eyebrows shot up in irritation, and her eyes narrowed with anger. Suddenly she didn't look so innocent—a small crack in the demon's mask.

"I get off at one," she told me. "Could you wait for me in the alley out back? I don't like to have to walk home by myself."

I checked the time. It was twelve thirty.

I flashed her broad grin. "I'll give you a ride, sweetheart."

She giggled and planted a little kiss on my cheek. I wanted to scrub it off, but I forced myself to be still. We returned to the club area, and Sasha dutifully headed for the stage, all smiles. Someone had snatched my seat while I was in the back with Sasha, and I plopped down on one of the bar stools. Onstage, Sasha began to seduce the rest of the club, but she continued to wink and flash me a few smiles.

I sported a smile of my own. I had scored a date with a demon.

For the next half hour, there was nothing to do but wait and watch. As I sipped on another Coors Light, I steeled myself for what lay ahead.

I experienced fear—what sane man wouldn't—but I refused to let the emotion control me. Instead, I put my trust into my training and drew confidence from it. I was a Marine. A SWAT commander. And now, a monster hunter.

This time, the succubus would be facing a different, much better-prepared opponent.

At five minutes before one, I paid my remaining tab at the bar and left the club. Near the entrance, sobs drifted through the night. They came from the jersey-wearing punk next to my motorcycle. From the looks of it, someone had gotten too frisky with my wheels. As the punk wailed about a mama who never breastfed him, I walked around the club and edged into the back alley.

The back of the club was dark and ugly and smelled of trash. Without the glittering neon to dazzle the senses, the place looked more like another abandoned warehouse in a shitty part of town than some pleasure palace. Talk about a fitting metaphor for the whole joint. Would the succubus try to kill me right here?

We would see...

I waited.

And waited.

After about fifteen minutes, I started to wonder if something might be wrong. Had the succubus seen through my magical disguise? Was my cover blown?

I was about to leave the shadowy alley and return to the club when the steel back door creaked open, and Sasha emerged. Her wholesome, innocent looks clashed with the squalid surroundings and the slick leather coat and long black boots she wore. Her eyes found me, and a smile brightened her angelic face.

I picked up a new emotion from her—hunger. It was subtle and barely noticeable to a regular person, but I was looking for any signs of the monster hiding under the mask. I had caught my first glimpse of the succubus, and it took all my willpower not to react.

*Patience*, I told myself. *You'll get your chance soon enough.*

Damn, I was starting to sound like Octurna.

Sasha stepped up to me and opened her coat. The move caught me momentarily off guard. I expected to see a naked body under the leather fabric. I'd imagined perky breasts and long, lean legs. Instead, her body consisted of a mass of snakelike arms which branched out like a blooming flower.

A second later, a tornado of whipping tentacles raced toward me.

I went for one of my silver daggers, but the monster's undulating limbs were faster. One wrapped around my hand. Another snaked around my neck and drew tight.

I gasped, choked and struggled for air.

Then the world turned dark, and the ground came rushing up at me.

## 9

My eyes screwed open, and I squinted, still groggy from the attack in the alley. As my vision adjusted to the low light, I realized I was back in the strip club. Hands cuffed to a steel chair on one of the dance stages. I caught my reflection in the wall of mirrors. Not surprisingly, my disguise had evaporated, and my own lean mug stared back at me. I no longer wore the cheap suit but sported my black monster hunting combat outfit. Unfortunately, my weapons were gone.

So much for the element of surprise.

No one in the joint paid me any mind, which struck me as odd. Their collective attention was riveted on the second, larger stage. Everybody in the club, all the way from the drooling horndogs to the 'roid-popping staff to Sasha's lingerie-clad sisters in arms, had gathered around.

The air crackled with anticipation. What was going on here?

I received the answer an instant later when a trending R & B song boomed from the speakers, and red and blue lights swept over the main stage. Sasha stood there, naked and lovely as my fantasy of her had been, surrounded by my arsenal. The submachine gun, my pistol, the daggers and gauntlet—they had all become props in her private little performance art piece.

She ran the silver daggers sensually over her bare flesh and blew me a kiss.

The demon was mocking me.

The whole club focused on Sasha as she started to writhe like a serpent around the steel pole, brandishing my weapons. One thing was for damn sure—my monster hunting career was getting off to a rocky start.

The succubus' moves hypnotized the hormonal crowd, her heat intoxicating. Even knowing what I did about her nature, I still couldn't pull my eyes away.

What was Sasha up to? Was she offering me one last dance before she finished me off?

She continued her mesmerizing performance, weaving a powerful spell over the club's patrons, working them all into a frenzy. I sensed that this was no ordinary dance. Her body glistened with sweat, her eyes afire as she took the burlesque arts to a new level. It rained bills on stage. Everyone watching would have eagerly parted with whatever fortune they had and would have gladly handed her the shirts of their backs if she so demanded.

I'd be willing to bet that they'd kill for her, too.

As soon as the thought crossed my mind, the music in the club died down. You could hear a pin drop in the place.

"Do you love me?" she asked the crowd, her tawny skin glowing in the spotlight, demanding to be touched. They held out their arms, prostrate with devotion. These weren't merely fans, they were her devoted followers. Her willing slaves.

"We love you, Sasha!" voices called out.

"Then prove it to me!"

A spotlight found me onstage, and Sasha leveled a long-nailed finger at me. The red nail polish looked like blood. The mob swiveled in my direction, angry eyes locking on me.

"This man tried to hurt me!"

With a single sentence, the succubus had turned yours truly into public enemy number one.

*Shit!*

The crowd closed in, eyes flashing with hatred, teeth bared. This wasn't looking good.

"Get him!" someone shouted.

The mob went nuts and stormed the stage. These fine folks were about to tear me apart with their bare hands. There would be no reasoning with the human tsunami.

Sasha let out a peal of triumphant laughter.

Fuck! I had to get off this stage. Out of this damn club. But last I checked, I couldn't break steel handcuffs.

Octurna's voice rang out in my head. She sounded almost scared. *"You're not the man you used to be, Jason. Dragon blood now runs through your veins. Now get up!"*

As the mob surged toward me, I tightened every muscle in my body, clenched my teeth and strained against the steel cuffs behind my back. Metal chafed away at my wrists as the first of my would-be executioners spilled onstage. My muscles erupted with a burst of power, and I roared with both pain and triumph as the metal gave way.

Not a moment too soon as a bouncer and a stripper tag teamed me. My fists came up, cuffs still wrapped around my wrists, and found their incoming faces. The impact sent them reeling, and they flew off the stage, making way for the next wave of Sasha's fan club. Judging from the way they glared at me, they sure as hell weren't here for a two-for-one special.

But neither was I.

I swirled toward the seething circle of humanity closing in on me, and my training kicked in. I was not looking to cripple or maim anyone—these people were victims themselves, their minds under the succubus's command, but neither could I let them rip me apart without putting up a fight.

My legs flashed out, arms snapping at the mob like

pistons. Fists and feet connected with devastating force as I barreled my way off stage. I had always enjoyed hand-to-hand combat; my jujitsu and Muay Thai skills having gotten me unscathed out of many a scrape over the years. The dragon blood cranked up my skill set to a whole other level—as these hapless fools were beginning to discover. I cut a devastating path through the throng, and I was still holding back.

I don't know how many teeth I knocked out before I dove off the stage. I landed behind the crowd, my long leather trench coat trailing behind me like a black cape. The club had transformed into a barroom brawl scene from some classic Western, the kind of movie my dad had loved and that they didn't make any more unless they featured robots or aliens.

My gaze ticked to the larger stage. Sasha was gone. She must've sensed the tides were turning. I swept the club and saw the succubus vanish in the back, apparently not willing to engage me in a direct fight. Coward.

I wanted her to know that I was coming after her. Wanted her to be afraid.

Never slowing down, I jumped onto the larger stage, tossing more of my attackers aside, and swiftly scooped up my guns and knives. She'd left me an arsenal. I wondered why Sasha hadn't just finished me off when she could have.

*"Luckily for you, succubi are narcissists,"* Octurna

explained. *They turn everything into a performance and have a fondness for the dramatic.*

Things were about to get a hell of lot more dramatic for the demon if I had a say in the matter.

Jaw set with growing irritation, I knocked a few more members of Sasha's personal fan club aside. They would wake up with a few extra bruises and possibly a broken heart but otherwise unharmed. On my way to the rear exit, I passed a few stunned female dancers who seemed to be the first ones to wake from Sasha's unholy trance. One of them was sobbing, but I didn't have time to care. I burst through the steel door. Now back in the alley, my head swiveled, eyes scoping, and I spotted Sasha vanishing around the corner of the dumpster-filled street.

The chase was on.

As I sprinted after the succubus, I vowed not to set foot in a titty bar ever again.

Within seconds, I reached the end of the alley and surged down the main street. The bouncer stared after me, his mouth hanging open. Between the shouts emanating from the club and a stripper being hunted down by a black-clad badass brandishing a glowing submachine gun straight out of a video game, the meathead took a step back and chose not to get involved.

Smart boy.

Sasha had a considerable head start, and she was edging further ahead with each passing second. She didn't seem to care who might see her superhuman speed at this point. She was probably running at fifty miles an hour. Even with dragon blood pumping through my body, I wouldn't be able to maintain this pace. I was falling behind.

I hated to admit it, but the succubus was getting away.

*"Don't let her escape, Jason. If she eludes you, she'll go underground. It'll take us weeks to find her."*

The urgency in Octurna's voice spurred me on and made me ignore my screaming lungs. I wondered why the sorceress cared so much about this particular demon. Killing the succubus and avenging my teammates meant a lot to me, but what was it to Octurna? The sorceress had referred to the demon as nothing more than a low-level thug, so why did it seem so important to her that I destroy her today? I doubted she was doing this for my emotional gratification. No, something else was going on here.

I pushed the questions aside and focused. How was I going to catch the fleeing demon? If only I had a magic-powered motorcycle...

A fierce grin spread across my face as I veered toward my bike, which was patiently waiting for me. I surged past the wannabe gangbanger who'd gotten a little too close to my ride earlier. He was still hugging himself tightly and rocking back and forth on the sidewalk, a shivering ball of humanity.

I swung onto the gleaming hunk of street bike, fired up

the engine and roared down the deserted street. The bike left me more vulnerable than a car but also provided greater maneuverability and faster acceleration. Plus, it was just *fun*.

I cranked up the speed, the bike's screaming engine cutting through the night as I shot underneath a freeway overpass. Traffic distantly roared overhead.

I saw the succubus vanish up ahead into a subway station. If I ditched my wheels and pursued her underground, I would soon lose her in the tunnels below.

I only had one option. Take the motorcycle with me.

Mind made up, I braced myself. My hands tightened around the *Nighthawk*'s handlebars, I slowed the bike a bit and then bounced down the subway stairs in dogged pursuit of my prey.

I wasn't letting her get away this time.

A few bone-rattling seconds later, the bike had completed its rapid-fire descent down the stairs and was now burning rubber across the subway platform. After the dark streets above, the brightly lit underground world felt blinding. A few late-night commuters gasped at the bike screaming past them, their mouths still open wide from seeing an almost-naked stripper running down that very same platform seconds earlier.

As the distance between me and my target continued to shrink, my eyes narrowed with anticipation. The moment of reckoning was drawing close. I couldn't wait.

The succubus reached the platform's edge, the dark tunnel yawning before her. She stole a glance back at me for a beat and then jumped off the platform. She landed on the deserted tracks with athletic grace and tore into the mouth of the shadow-drenched tunnel.

I cursed under my breath. I'd been hoping to catch up with her before she disappeared inside the tunnel system.

No such luck.

I cranked up the engine and raced after, a madman on a mission. The platform's edge came up, the endless tunnel system opening up before me. My whole body braced for impact as the motorcycle flew off the subway platform and sailed out into space.

I arced through the darkness, remained airborne a few heart-stopping feet, carried by sheer momentum, before my bike slammed into the tracks below with an explosive crack.

Sparks exploded from under the frame as I desperately fought for control of my ride. For a moment, *Nighthawk* felt a bit wobbly before I succeeded in steadying the bike. My ultra-fast, dragon-blood-enhanced reflexes were paying off.

Up ahead, the succubus began to slow down, perhaps sensing that escape had ceased to be an option. The creature would have to confront me.

Finally.

I gunned the throttle, and the heavy bike blasted after the succubus at full bore.

And that's when another sound drowned out the roar of my motorcycle. Flashing headlights jumped into view, and I swallowed hard. Barreling toward at me breakneck speed was a subway train.

A devious smile curled the lips of the succubus as the creature vanished in the shadows. The demon had known the incoming train was her best bet at getting away from me.

*"Keep going,"* Octurna said.

*Well, I wish I could, but there is the matter of the train that's about to run me over.*

I eased the throttle, planning to make a U-turn as soon as I slowed down enough.

*"Keep heading for the train. The magic of the bike will protect you!"*

"Are you fucking crazy?" I said out loud.

*"Trust me, Jason."*

Octurna was asking a lot here. But she hadn't spent the last month whipping me into shape to see me get run over by a subway train before this magical war even got started.

To my surprise, I did trust the sorceress. At least when it came to matters of personal survival. I wasn't stupid. I sensed Octurna was keeping things from me, holding back information. But she wouldn't sacrifice me for no reason.

I cranked the engine and shot like a bolt of lightning toward the oncoming train.

The headlights grew larger and larger. They became my world, a blinding vortex of light.

I had died once. I wasn't afraid to do it again. My lips twisted into a determined snarl, and I fired the bike into the roaring train at full tilt.

If I was wrong about this...well, best not to think about it.

Just as I was about to hit the mechanized monster, the bike surged with spectral energy and enveloped me in a protective bubble of green light, a sharp reminder that the *Nighthawk* was far from an ordinary bike. This was a magical motorcycle. Flames ignited around the madly spinning tires.

I screamed. Hey, you would too.

To my stunned relief, the devastating collision I expected never materialized. The train warped around me for a split second, and then both the bike and I grew transparent and phased out of reality. For a few stunned beats, I was passing through one car after another as if I was a ghost, having become as insubstantial as smoke.

Magic had only recently become part of my world, and I sensed this was just the tip of the iceberg. I was now part of a new reality where the old rules and limitations didn't apply.

All these thoughts raced through my mind as the train

rippled through me at breakneck speed. Now that I had committed myself to the act, the fear drained away from me, and I experienced a deep calm. I caught glimpses of bored late-night commuters slumped in their seats. Most were dozing or on their phones, unaware of the miracle playing out around them. I was invisible to them, and I was glad for their sakes. Witnessing some ghost motorcyclist on a moving train would have been a hard image to shake even for the most open-minded individual. Maybe you could get away with that shit in San Francisco, but this was L.A.

And then the rush of subway cars stopped, and I was back in the dimly lit tunnel, going sixty-five miles per hour. I stole a quick glance back and saw the train continuing on its way as if nothing had happened. The *Nighhawk* stopped glowing, its color returning to normal.

I grinned like a little kid. I was alive.

My happy mood didn't last as a shadow darted from the darkness, moving with a life of its own.

With horror, I watched as the shape elongated and shot out at me with serpentine speed. My tattoos lit up with power. The fast-moving form rammed into me and lifted me out of my seat, sending me flying. I spun through the tunnel and landed face down on the tracks. Hard. The impact sent the air out of my lungs, and I nearly spit up my last meal. I groaned with pain, but all my limbs were still working.

A hissing sound echoed through the tunnel, and I scrambled back to my feet.

My eyes widened in disgust and fear as I got a good look at the attacking succubus. Sasha had taken on what I assumed was her true form. A monster that was half snake, half sex goddess now reared up at me. Just looking at her made my skin crawl.

From the torso up, the succubus was all woman, beautiful features, full breasts, and perfect skin, but from the waist down, I was looking at the body of a fearsome snake. This was a beast of myth, a nightmare from another age, straight from the deepest pits of Hell.

It was both repellent...and seductive. That was the crazy part. I now understood how Sasha had been so flexible on stage, her agile suppleness making sense to me. A long snake tongue shot from the sensual lips, revealing rows of razor-sharp teeth. My stomach twisted with revulsion as the creature homed in on me.

The succubus hissed again, and a toxic cloud engulfed me. For one eternal moment nothing much happened, and then the effects kicked in, and I couldn't breathe.

Another satisfied smile lit up those sweet, innocent-looking features as the snake woman inexorably slithered toward me.

My hand whipped out one of the silver daggers from my bandolier and rammed it into her bare human torso. She recoiled with another hiss, triumph giving way to pain. My other hand reached for the 9mm and unloaded into the demon. Silver bullets stitched the serpent body, and it flailed wildly on the tracks.

I was hurting the succubus. But despite the stab and bullet wounds, the beast was still full of life. I made the sign of the circle, and the air warped and rippled as a beam of concentrated magical energy tore into the monster. The bolt ripped a big chunk out of the snake woman's body, painting the tracks black with demon blood.

*"You must take her head,"* Octurna told me. *"That's the only way. Use your gauntlet.*

The twin blades shot out of the gauntlet with an audible snap. The subway tunnel's halogen lights sparkled on the cold steel. Both knives now pointed at the succubus. She looked up at me, batting those big eyes, and for just a moment I was looking at sweet little Sasha again.

"Don't, please," she said, her voice shaking.

*"Stop hesitating and slay the beast!"*

I brought the gauntlet's blades down on the creature. I almost expected the steel to bounce off the demon's thick, coarse skin. Instead, the blades sliced through the succubus's neckline like butter, separating the head in one fell swoop. The headless body reared up with a final burst of energy before it collapsed lifelessly over the tracks.

*"Well done, my knight. I knew you could do it."*

I wiped the blood and sweat off my face, somewhat surprised by my victory. And that's when the tattoos all over my body came alive. The burning sensation built in intensity. I gasped, stunned by the pain searing through my entire being. The agony felt disturbingly familiar, and for a second, I flashed back to that fateful night when Octurna transferred some of her magic to me. It felt like I was being tattooed all over again. What the hell was happening now?

My eyes grew large as I received a hint of the answer.

The snake creature lit up with reddish energy. As the slain demon dissolved into nothingness, waves of red energy shot from its dead form and passed into my body. Into my tattoos.

Understanding slashed through my mind. I was absorbing the demon's energy. It took all my self-control not to scream. If another train came down the tracks now, I would be done for.

I hunched over, wracked with agony. I felt like I was burning alive. Had flames erupted from my tats, I wouldn't have been surprised. And then, as rapidly as the initial burst of pain had passed through me, my tingling nerve endings calmed down. I sucked in air and just lay there for a beat, a shaking bag of Jell-o.

*"You must get up. Hurry. It's vital that you return to the Sanctuary as soon as possible."*

The urgency in Octurna's voice forced me to my feet.

The body of the succubus was gone, having evaporated into thin air.

*"Not thin air. Magical energy. Energy that belongs to you. To us."*

I shook off the cobwebs and searched the dark tunnel for my motorcycle. I had expected to find it crashed against one of the tunnel walls, a wreck of mangled steel, but nothing could be further from the truth. The cycle stood a few feet away, engine purring. It had kept on going even without its rider and performed a sharp U-turn. I stared at the green-glowing bike. Would the miracles ever cease?

*"Aren't you forgetting something?"* Octurna asked.

"What is it now?"

*"Bring me the head of the beast!"*

Had I heard correctly? Did Octurna want the demon's head?

*"Bring me my trophy, night slayer. Hurry!"*

I didn't like the sharp, demanding tone that had crept into Octurna's voice. Was there even a skull to bring back? As far as I could tell, the succubus had gone supernova.

*"The body of a slain demon becomes light and fire and turns to ash, but the head remains,"* Octurna explained. *"Search the area. It will be nearby.*

I reluctantly complied, and within seconds spotted the dead monster's head. Eerily enough, the creature's preternatural beauty remained preserved in death, the expression on her face serene. I grimaced and fought back a wave of revulsion. As I reached for the head and lifted it into the air, a burst of red energy emanated from my tattoos and melted the skin and hair away, reducing it to bone and enamel. My throat tight with shock and disgust, I held the monster's bleached skull out at arm's length.

*"Don't tell me the warriors of the twenty-first century are too squeamish to take trophies of their slain enemies?"*

I sighed. I was in no mood to argue with the sorceress about the conventions of modern-day military conflicts. The tracks started to rattle—the next train was coming, and I took it as my cue to get the hell out of here.

I jammed the skull in the *Nighthawk*'s tail bag. I straddled the motorcycle, squeezed the clutch and thumbed the ignition. I leaped from the shadows and hurtled down the subway tunnel.

## 10

I was still following the line of subway tracks when a familiar rumbling sound grew audible. A subway car was gaining behind me. As much fun as my first ghost ride through a moving train had been, I wasn't all too keen on repeating the experience. Besides, I worried the magical energy powering the bike had its limits. What if I failed to phase out on the second round? No, best I get out of the subway as fast as possible.

"*Take the tunnel to your left,*" Octurna piped up in my mind.

My eye scoped my surroundings, and I detected waves of light emanating from a narrow maintenance tunnel that intersected with the main tracks. I could have sworn it hadn't been there a few moments ago. As I powered into the passageway, my suspicion was confirmed. The narrow side tunnel led straight into the Sanctuary. The fortress had materialized right inside the Los Angeles subway system.

A heartbeat later, I came to a grinding stop in front of Octurna's black throne. The *Nighthawk*'s tires smoked, the engine belched, and the bike's green magical fire died down. I shot a glance backward and saw the next subway train rattle past the giant arched window right before the familiar bank of stained-glass windows replaced the image. Even though I now I lived in a world where wonders were quickly becoming commonplace, I still felt a thrill. It would take a long time for me to get used to such miracles. I was ways off from becoming jaded as far as magic was concerned.

My gaze turned to the shadowy figure ensconced in the black-carved throne. I let out an audible gasp at what I saw there. As I approached the sorceress, I realized she had changed...and not for the better. The creature meeting my searching expression shared very little in common with the seductive, ivory-skinned beauty who haunted my thoughts. The face had sunken in, the bones sharp underneath the shriveled flesh, the mane of raven-black hair now the color of snow. Gone were her curves, the red robe draped over a skeletal frame. The hint of red tattoos against tight, supple flesh, once so entrancing, now looked like lines of blood etched on a living corpse. Only the magnetic green eyes remained the same in those wizened features.

"What happened? What's wrong with you?"

No answer was forthcoming. Octurna's bony fingers waved me closer. As in a trance I obeyed. Prey walking into the spider's web.

And then those ebony fingers closed around my wrist with surprising strength, and my tattoos came alive. Energy rippled through my body, my lips contorted with pain, and I barely stifled the scream desperate to claw its way out of my throat.

Octurna's own tattoos blazed with power. The red lines of ink brightened and pulsated with renewed energy as my tats faded in color and grew dimmer.

She was feeding on the energy, I realized. Like some kind of vampire.

Pain shot through every fiber of my being as the power transfer continued unchecked between us. And as the complex network of ink intensified in color and became blinding, the magic restored Octurna's beauty. Her face filled in, the loose folds of wrinkled skin grew taut, the white hair turned black again. I watched in wonder as the hag transformed into the mesmerizing beauty who had changed the course of my life.

The pain stopped, and Octurna released me from her iron grip.

I recoiled. The sorceress' back was straight and regal, her posture perfect, projecting strength and vitality. She was back in control, her magic and looks restored.

"Thank you, Jason. And I'm sorry you had to see this."

"What *are* you?" I asked in a low voice.

Octurna rose from her throne with a teasing smile.

"My power is limited, another side effect of the death spell. That bike of yours runs on magic. Your spells require magic. Guess who generates that magical energy?"

I stared at her while I tried to untangle her words. "So what are you saying, you're like a magical battery?"

"Close enough."

It made sense. The tattoos on my body were a receiver for Octurna's mystical energy. I was learning how to tap into that power and cast spells, but it was all fueled by the sorceress's magic in the end. The same held true for my new bike and all my monster hunting gear.

Octurna nodded at the bag on my bike. "Would you be a dear and hand over my prize?"

Her prize? Momentary confusion gave way to understanding. Octurna was referring to the succubus's skull.

Slowly, I turned to the cycle. I popped the back case and removed the demon's skull. Octurna almost greedily accepted the trophy and held it high above her head, her eyes now smoldering with a dark fire. I recognized that look. I was pretty sure I sported a similar expression when I slew the demon, and it scared the shit out of me.

Skull in hand, the sorceress marched toward the nearest pedestal and placed it on one of the display tables where it joined the dragon, vampire, and werewolf skulls.

Her lips stretched into a smile with no hint of amusement. "Soon enough, this chamber will fill with the skulls of our slain enemies. This is only the beginning."

I considered these words in contemplative silence.

"You were after the demon's magical power," I said after a long pause. "That's why you sent me after the succubus and not after one of the seven magical big bads."

"Their turn will come. You wouldn't stand a chance against the seven at your current power level. Do you want to win this war or become an early casualty?"

Lightning fast, Octurna vanished into thin air and appeared right behind me, her hand clutched around my throat. With horror, I realized that half her ghostlike arm was inside of my chest. I clenched my jaw, determined not to scream. There was something perversely intimate about the horrific act, about her nearness. I could feel her skin against mine, smell her sweet fragrance, and almost taste her.

"Your powers are growing, Jason, and you're a formidable soldier, but if we hope to score future victories, we'll have to take things slowly, one battle at a time, one trophy at a time. Both you and I need to become stronger. And the more magical beings we slay, the more power we will gain. Do you understand?"

"Yes," I said.

"Good." Octurna withdrew her arm from inside my body, and I clutched my chest.

"With each kill, you will restore my power, but your own abilities will grow too. New spells will become available, spells that will allow us to face the leaders of the Shadow Cabal."

"And what if I'm done with all this craziness?" I said defiantly. I hated feeling like the pawn in someone else's game. And I felt betrayed by Octurna on some level. Why hadn't she told me about her need to feed on magic? What other secrets was she keeping from me? Besides a sick proclivity for collecting trophies of her enemies, that is.

"You might be done, but this war isn't done with you. Do you really think you could return to your old life knowing what you know?"

I didn't answer.

Octurna continued, "You're no pawn, Jason and this is your game as much as it's mine. If the seven dark masters succeed, mankind will descend in darkness and chaos. More innocent lives will perish. We must stop the Shadow Cabal."

She eased closer, moving like silk, her voice a glassy whisper. "I thought you wanted to make a difference, Jason. This is your chance."

She was right, damn it. I couldn't go back even if the world hadn't buried me already. This was my war, too. I was just smarting over Octurna keeping me in the dark. I had to get over my bruised ego and keep the bigger picture in mind.

"Okay, I get it. Baby steps," I said. "Kill one monster at a time, build a lovely skull collection, level up."

Octurna's lips stretched into a genuine smile. "I'm glad we understand each other, Jason. Now if you need some relaxation after your last adventure…"

On cue, Nuala and Zemira peeled from the shadows. They both tilted their heads in my direction, the invitation to follow them unmistakable, but I wasn't in the mood for another round of freaky fun with a couple of magical love dolls.

"I wouldn't call them that," Octurna said. "They might take it the wrong way."

I glared at Octurna. Could she read every one of my thoughts?

"Let's stop playing around." I fixed my gaze on the windows. "With the succubus out of the picture, what's our next move?"

"Sounds like someone is eager to risk his life again." Octurna dramatically reclined on her throne and regarded the stained-glass windows. "Do you think those kids managed to conjure a succubus without receiving direction from someone more familiar with the dark arts?"

I shrugged. "Honestly, I didn't give it much thought. I figured they picked it up by playing Dungeons & Dragons."

The sorceress cocked an eyebrow, clearly not getting the reference.

"Never mind," I said. "So how did those kids pull this deadly magic trick off?"

"Someone used their natural curiosity and anger and channeled it into an occult ritual."

One of the windows now offered a glimpse into the past. I saw goth kids gathered in a circle. They were performing the ceremony which would thrust the sex demon into our reality. Little did they know they wouldn't live to see the next morning.

"The girl leading the ritual and all her friends were students at USC," Octurna said.

I shot the sorceress a disbelieving look. "Don't tell me they were taking Witchcraft 101."

"Not witchcraft, but History of Magic and Ritual taught by Professor Robert Brogan."

I stepped closer to the observation windows. Peering through the magical portal, I watched a swarm of bright young college kids rush into a campus lecture building.

"And you think this Professor Brogan told them to conjure a demon for homework?"

"Very funny. Joke as much as you like, but Brogan is the likeliest suspect."

I wasn't convinced. "What if these kids just wanted to spice up a Friday night by dabbling with the dark side? I hear it beats the club scene."

"These kids didn't *dabble*," Octurna said sharply, not amused. "They unleashed true evil into our world. That is something you can't just pick up from reading a book. You need to know what you're doing. Someone with a real understanding of black magic helped them."

"Okay," I said, holding up my hands.

"I understand and even respect your skepticism. But there's more. Other incidents over the years connected to the campus. In 2016, sophomore Janet Welch murdered her boyfriend by stabbing him thirty times before committing acts of cannibalism."

"Jesus."

"Friends described them as madly in love."

I shook my head. "Emphasis on *madly*."

"According to police reports, the court statements, and psychiatric evaluations, she claimed she was possessed by a demon."

"Let me guess, she was a USC student taking Professor Brogan's class."

"How ever did you know?" Octurna said sarcastically.

"Alright, cut it out, and just keep going. You've got more?"

Octurna nodded sagely. "The list goes on and on. Every occult crime committed in the last ten years in Los Angeles by a young person..."

"Leads back to the good professor," I finished. "Okay, so what are you saying? The teacher gets off by feeding young people to demons?"

"Something like that. My guess is Brogan is an acolyte,

a fledgling member of the Shadow Cabal who is earning his stripes."

"So why corrupt these kids? What does he gain from a succubus running around LA?"

Impatience tinged Octurna's voice as she answered. "I believe the Cabal is readying this world for a terrible spell, a spell that will draw on the negative emotions of every person on this planet."

I mulled this over. It made a terrible kind of sense. "So the worse things get, the easier it is to pull this super-spell off?"

"You're beginning to understand. Slowly."

I shifted back to the image of the busy school campus. Among the frolicking students glued to their phones or chattering away with friends, without a care in the world, a new figure emerged. The man was bald, with a black goatee that matched his dark designer suit. He wore a golden necklace with a five-pointed star pendant. His icy eyes observed the milling crowd, his features empty of all emotion.

"He sure looks the part of a wannabe occultist."

Octurna gave a dismissive sniff. "Acolytes tend to overcompensate as they try to prove themselves to the Cabal and earn a place in the organization."

The stained-glass window zeroed in on Brogan, and this time I noticed a black tattoo on his neck. It showed an inverted triangle inside a circle.

"He carries the mark of an acolyte," Octurna said. "His presence in this city means that a Cabal lodge must be nearby."

"Lodge? You mean like a freemason thing?"

She shrugged. "The Shadow Cabal has its agents all over the world in all the major cities. The lodges act as informal headquarters and centers of power, hidden bases so to speak."

I kept studying the man, beginning to grasp the enormity of the task we'd set for ourselves. We were not going up against a few monsters here, but a magical mafia. A secret society not driven by violence and greed but a desire to destroy the world as we know it.

The sorceress moved toward me silently and placed a slender hand on my arm. "Ready to go back to school, Jason?"

## 11

I faced the wall of stained glass windows, eager to venture into the real world again. After all, I was still craving that In-And-Out burger. But I had some questions first.

I turned to Octurna. "How come your windows can't track the good professor to the lodge?"

Octurna sighed. "I wish it was that simple. The whereabouts of their lodges are secret and protected by wards and other magical defense systems."

"So you want me to make contact with Brogan and follow him back to his evil lair?"

The sorceress shook her head. "No, much too risky. If Brogan catches on that he is being followed, we lose our chance at locating the lodge. I have a better idea. Give me your hand."

I hesitated for a moment but complied. What other

choice did I have? Octurna leaned forward, and I gently opened my hand and turned it toward her, so the palm was facing up. Her touch was electric, and my breath hitched in my throat. Even though I'd seen her before the black magic makeover, I still found the sorceress utterly bewitching.

"Relax. This will sting a bit."

I sighed inwardly. Why did it always have to *sting* when we made physical contact?

I inhaled, breathing in her scent. She smelled of soap and musk and fresh grass, and I was having a hard time not thinking of our first encounter on the altar...

A sharp pain pulled me out of my semi-erotic daydream. Octurna had used one of her long fingernails to prick the palm of my hand, drawing blood. And now she was using that same bloody fingernail to carve an oval shape into my outstretched hand. My blood gleamed in the glow of the flickering stained-glass windows.

My first instinct was to whip my bleeding hand back, but Octurna waved her other finger at me, her magnetic gaze ordering me to stay put. To trust her. There was a method to her madness. At least I hoped so. The circle of blood on my palm solidified and turned into scar tissue. It resembled an eye with a scraggly line below it.

"I assume this a spell of some kind?" I asked when she at last released me.

"The eye will let you track Brogan. All you have to do is

shake his hand and mark him with the all-seeing Eye of Horus."

I stared at my new scar, not convinced.

"Don't worry about the mark. As soon as you transfer the spell to the target, your hand will return to normal."

"That's a reassuring thought."

"Professor Brogan's class should start in about ten minutes. And he hates it when people show up late. Especially folks who aren't officially enrolled."

The windows started to blur together and morphed into one enormous stained-glass pane that showed the red brick buildings that made up the USC campus. The glass shimmered and once again became a doorway into reality.

Octurna nodded, and I stepped through the gateway.

Three determined steps later, and I found myself on the bustling campus. I gasped but managed the unnerving sensations of cold and terror that accompanied the portal jump. My presence didn't earn any strange looks from the flocks of students, and I figured my magic had already altered my outward appearance. A quick glance at my reflection in the nearest window confirmed that much—I was now wearing a pair of well-worn Converse and ragged skinny jeans with a blue hoodie draped over a beanpole physique. I was about as non-threatening as you can get. I was almost scared to catch a better look at my face and find some pimple-faced mug staring back at me.

Magic was a trip. Talk about the understatement of the year.

I caught a few coeds smiling at me, so my latest disguise wasn't completely unappealing to the members of the opposite sex this time around.

*"Focus on the mission, Jason."*

*Jealous?*

I turned and saw the sorceress standing in the doorway of a building that blended with the rest of the campus. I noticed a few students glancing at this new structure curiously, on some level registering that something was wrong, but unable to pinpoint the problem and break through the haze of Octurna's magic. Most just shrugged and went about their day. No one tried to explore the mystery building more closely, subconsciously sensing that it was off limits.

*"Run along now, Slayer. You don't want to be late for your first day of school."*

I grinned at the good-natured jab, resisted the impulse to give the sorceress the finger, and was on my merry way.

I studied the college kids the way an anthropologist would examine a new species of hominid. I felt cut off from their carefree lives. They only had to worry about tests and getting laid, while I battled to save the world from an occult conspiracy. I had fought in two military conflicts, and now I was waging a private war with some secret cabal of magicians. It was hard to believe that my reality and theirs might intersect in any significant way, that sheltered academia could collide with a world of magic and monsters. But an agent of chaos had invaded this school, hellbent on corrupting young, impressionable minds. Professor Brogan's dark influence had directly led to the deaths of my closest friends, and I was eager to make his acquaintance.

Determined, I approached the social science building and joined the group of students streaming through the doors, on their way to the lecture hall where Brogan held court three times a week. The auditorium was enormous and fit about four hundred students. This wasn't some intimate gathering, which was both good and bad. Good because the professor most likely wouldn't notice a newcomer; bad because it might prove more challenging to strike up a conversation after class.

I took a seat and watched the professor with growing interest. A few details became clear rather quickly once he started his lecture. Brogan was good at his job. I mean *really good*. Like everyone, I had my fair share of bad teachers growing up, but Professor Brogan wouldn't have been one of them. Funny, personable and he knew how to keep things exciting and engaging at all times, drawing from a wide range of disciplines during his lecture. He would touch on history, psychology, anthropology, art, and social studies, making sure everything he said was relevant to the lives of his students. I found myself getting swept up in his spiel despite myself. An hour later, I had picked up some fascinating facts about occult masks and the role they played in religious ritual—and how we all wore masks to one degree or another.

*And sometimes we wear masks to get closer to our enemies*, I thought.

As the students filed out of the hall, I made my way to the lectern, intent to shake the man's hand under some pretense that wouldn't arouse suspicion.

Brogan was busy packing his class materials in a leather satchel. A few girls swarmed around him, using the pretext of some upcoming assignment to chat him up. It was rapidly becoming clear to me how the professor had managed to steer his students toward the darkness. This wasn't some creepy old man who spent his days alone in libraries or skulking in back alleys. Brogan was attractive and charming, an academic with rock star appeal. The Shadow Cabal had chosen their agent well.

I pushed all these thoughts aside, abruptly worried that I might be dealing with a mind-reader like Octurna.

*"I wouldn't worry about that, slayer. Like yourself, the good professor has only begun his black magic journey. He won't be able to probe your thoughts...and if he should try, our magic will keep him at bay."*

*I'll take your word for it,* I thought. It was more than enough having just one person tuned in to my thoughts.

I flashed the professor a plastic smile and extended my

hand. "Professor Brogan, my name is John. It's an honor to meet you. My friends have been bugging me to check out your class. I will definitely be enrolling next semester."

For a moment, Brogan regarded me with a startled expression and then shook my hand. "I hope to see you in the fall, then."

"You can count on it."

Brogan still eyed me with that puzzled look before two smiling female students demanded his attention. Their timing was perfect. High time to cut a hasty exit. It hadn't been my best performance but the best I could come up with on short notice. I had always been better at banging down doors than subterfuge. But I was a fast learner.

I stealthily glanced at my hand. As Octurna had promised earlier, the scar was gone.

*"Well done, Jason. Now get out of there before Brogan gets suspicious."*

For once I was in total agreement with the sorceress. I rushed out of the lecture hall and headed for the exit of the social science building. A few minutes later I was on my way back to the mysterious new building that had materialized on the campus grounds.

As soon as I stepped inside, the double-doors transformed into a wall of stained-glass again, and I was back in Octurna's fortress.

"Good job," she said with a smile. "Now let's see how

the professor likes to spend his day when he is not teaching black magic tricks to his students."

I shifted my gaze to the stained-glass windows. They were now tracking the professor as he navigated the campus. After watching Brogan eat his lunch in the school cafeteria for a half an hour and surfing the web for another twenty minutes in the faculty room, I'd had enough of this mystical live-cam business.

Octurna must have noticed my bored expression, because she said, "You better get some rest. I'll let you know if things should get interesting."

She didn't have to repeat those words. My sluggish body seemed to have developed a will of its own as I dragged my tired ass back to my sleeping quarters. I guessed the fight with the succubus had taken more out of me than I initially realized. As I made my way out of the observation room, I saw the two golems watching me from the shadows. Their faceless features flickered and morphed into the two stunning beauties I had spent the night with. There was a playful, coquettish twinkle in their eyes as they winked at me. I was tempted to take them up on the silent offer, but in the end I averted my gaze. Last night had been fun, but I felt exhausted after my little lap dance from hell with the succubus. Maybe I was getting old.

Once in my bedchamber, I tossed my coat across a

chair and lay down. By the time my head hit the pillows, I was fast asleep.

I don't know how long I was out before Octurna's constructs shook me awake. Minutes or hours might have passed—there was no way to tell. Time had long lost its meaning inside the Sanctuary. Peering up at the constructs, I bolted out of bed before they could mistake my morning wood for an invitation. They were back to their faceless forms and didn't inspire any X-rated thoughts in me.

I nodded groggily and rose to my feet. The two golems watched me in silence as I got dressed. I wondered again what these creatures were. Did they have feelings and their own thoughts, or were they the equivalent of magical drones under Octurna's command?

"You guys don't say much, do you?" I grumbled.

"Conversation is overrated, don't you think?" one of the golems said and transformed into a darkly tanned Filipina who reminded me of a fling I'd once had during my military years abroad. I treasured the memories of that brief erotic encounter to this day. The robe slipped off the woman's shoulders, revealing the tight physique of a sun-kissed fitness girl. Perky tits, a tight ass, smooth skin. I swallowed hard, my mouth going dry.

I was still staring, debating if this was Nuala or Zemira, when the second golem stripped off her hooded robe, revealing a full-figured, luscious Latina beauty. Her petite yet voluptuous body made me think of Salma Hayek in *From Dusk to Dawn*. Damn, I'd watched that scene with the snake dance more times than I liked to admit. Was the sorceress probing my mind for sexual fantasies?

*Don't overthink it, Jason. We are at war, and each day might be your last. Enjoy the pleasures life gives you. You never know when it could all be taken away.*

Octurna made some good points, almost as if she was talking from personal experience. But I wondered why she didn't join the fun herself. Why was she using magical proxies for these sexual encounters? I'd have been more than happy to welcome her into my bed.

The sorceress refused to provide me with an answer. Maybe she was more of a voyeur. Or maybe she was afraid to let her guard down. It had to be hard, being a military general in this new war. Was she afraid of losing her objectivity if we allowed ourselves to get too close.

Or maybe I was just fooling myself.

The two beauties circled me. "So who's who now?" I eyed the Latina beauty. "Are you Nuala or Zemira?"

"Does it matter?" she asked. "You can call us anything you like."

As attracted as I was, a part of me grew cold. Maybe if I had been sixteen, this would have been enough. But I liked to get to know the women I spent my nights with. And even though the constructs could technically become anyone, who were they deep down? I almost expected the sorceress to invade my thoughts again and tell me that I was no fun, but she stayed out of my head or at least held her peace.

These questions were still going through my mind when the Filipina exchanged a deep, passionate kiss with her Latina partner. In the end, I was a just man. And these vixens were determined to drive me crazy. The Asian goddess pulled away from her friend and kneeled before me, her delicate fingers closing around my raging hard-on. I moaned with pleasure and my mind went blank.

All too soon, I would have to risk my life again. This could be my last day on Earth. Better to seize and enjoy the moment. Right?

## 12

An hour later, feeling refreshed and ready to take on the entire Shadow Cabal single-handed, I stepped up to Octurna's rough-hewn stone throne. There was something eerie about the way she surveyed her collection of monster skulls, her medieval throne bathed in the eerie red and blue light generated by her stained-glass windows. Part Disney villainess, part femme fatale from a *Heavy Metal* comic strip.

Did she spend her nights glued to the windows or did she retire to some shadowy tomb inside her fortress? What else did she do besides pore over ancient occults texts? What did she do for fun?

These questions and more cycled through my mind, making me realize how little I knew about my new partner. And how much I wanted to get to know her better.

"I hope you have a good reason for interrupting my beauty sleep," I said good-naturedly.

The sorceress's emerald eyes sparked, and her lips stretched into a triumphant smile as she said, "We have the location of the Cabal's lodge."

I followed Octurna's gaze to the bank of stained-glass windows. Their patterns focused on a black BMW as it made its way up a winding mountain road. Two other luxury cars trailed the first vehicle. The window zoomed into the BMW, revealing the by now familiar face of the driver—it was none other than Professor Brogan.

The window pulled away and showed the BMW's destination. The car was headed for a sprawling, palatial estate that grew from a lush, forested mountain. The property vaguely recalled a medieval castle or chateau with its towers and turrets as it reigned atop a promontory, dark and foreboding like a storm cloud. The place must have cost a frigging fortune, and I could only imagine how spectacular the views were.

"I thought these cult guys like to keep a low profile."

"Sometimes they choose to hide in plain sight. You're looking at the headquarters of the New Magic Center, a quasi-religious organization giving Scientology a run for its money. Their slogan is 'bring magic back into your life.'"

"Wow. I bet showbiz types are eating it up."

Octurna nodded. "The Shadow Cabal loves to recruit

from the elite, the famous, and affluent."

"Sure looks like they found some well-heeled donors. If you tell me my favorite stars are part this, I'm calling for a timeout."

Octurna narrowed her eyes and drummed her fingers on the ebony armrests of her throne. Her impatience was palpable, and I decided to tone down the jokes. My face grew serious as I shifted my attention back to the fortress-like estate filling up the large window. I watched with interest as the BMW pulled up to the mansion's parting wrought-iron gate.

Damn, this magical tracking spell was paying off big time! I was impressed and humbled by Octurna's abilities. If she could pull this kind of stuff off in her weakened state, what was a full-blown mage capable off? It was best not to think about it too much.

Suddenly, the window zapped out of existence, turning back to a wall of stained-glass. Someone had cut off our tracking spell.

"What happened? Did Brogan realize we're keeping tabs on him?"

Octurna shook her head. "My tracking spell was crafted to avoid detection and disperse at the first sign of a magical defense system. The Eye of Horus has served its purpose well. We located the lodge. It's up to you now, slayer."

*No pressure.*

The sorceress grinned, leaning forward on her throne. "I hope you're well rested, because you're about to work up a sweat."

There was no double entendre to Octurna's words—unfortunately, she wasn't teasing another encounter with her two magical servants. The workout that awaited me was of a very different nature.

"You want me to go scorched earth on that place?"

"I want you to burn it down to the ground, slayer. Think you're up for the challenge?"

"Only one way to find out. We'll need some serious explosive power to bring a place this size down. I hoped you stocked up on Semtex."

Octurna shook her head. "Who needs such crude weapons when you have magic at your disposal?"

The sorceress extricated a red-glowing crystal ball from her robe. It radiated a menacing glow and looking right at it hurt my eyes.

"Your mission is simple. Infiltrate the mansion. Head to the center of the property. And shatter this crystal ball."

I hung back slightly. "Are you telling me that's a magical bomb?"

The devilish smile plastered on Octurna's face told me everything I needed to know.

"I assume this isn't a suicide mission, so how long do I have to get out of there once I crack the egg?"

"About three minutes."

"Piece of cake," I said with more confidence than I really felt. Who knew what magical or monstrous surprises were waiting for me in the Cabal lodge? Plus, carrying around a magical super-explosive wasn't my idea of fun.

"We're about to send a message to the Shadow Cabal," Octurna said with dark satisfaction. "I want them to receive it loud and clear."

I shifted my attention to the cache of monster slaying weaponry and started to arm myself for the mission. I slung the bandolier of silver daggers over my shoulder, slipped on the shoulder holster with my 9mm and snapped on the monster slayer gauntlet. The twin blades shot out with an audible snap, the red light of the stained-glass windows playing over the razor-sharp steel, a preview of the upcoming carnage. I grabbed the submachine gun and fixed my gaze on the estate again.

I was ready to do this. As ready as I'd ever be.

"Remember your training. And don't get cocky. Reconnoiter, infiltrate, destroy and high tail it out of there."

"I sure like the sound of the last part of your plan."

Octurna shot me a long, almost disapproving look. "Sometimes I wonder if I made the right choice when I recruited you for this crusade."

"It's called having a sense of humor, babe. You should try it some time."

"This isn't like any enemy you faced in your past, Jason.

We're not in Afghanistan or Iraq."

"I know. But I used to play *World of Warcraft*, too. And I was pretty good at it."

The sorceress cocked an eyebrow, once more not getting the reference. I usually was the one playing catch up, so it was nice to see our roles reversed for a change.

"This is real war, Jason."

"I'm a marine. This is not the first time I've stared death in the face."

Octurna handed me the crimson crystal. Perspiration beaded my forehead as I gently accepted the red crystal ball. I pocketed the magical bomb, treating it with the greatest care, almost as if I was handling a volatile beaker of nitroglycerin.

"Don't worry. It's not going to break if you drop it, slayer. Only a magical blast can shatter the crystal."

"Thanks for telling me now." A strange heat had enveloped my whole body when I touched the bomb, its power undeniable. My gaze landed on *the Nighthawk*, which revved to life, the bike sensing a new mission was imminent. Like the golems, my new ride seemed to have a degree of awareness.

Sometimes it felt like my life had become an X-rated version of *Fantasia*.

Before I could have any second thoughts, I was astride my ride and blasting through the portal. Cold darkness gripped me, and my bowels tightened as I crossed the invisible threshold between the pocket dimension and the real world. Nausea hit my stomach like a dump truck. And then the sensation passed, and I found myself in the Malibu mountains, fading scarlet sunlight dappling the beautiful hillsides, the blue of the Pacific a thin band in the distance stretching into smoggy infinity.

The wheels of my motorcycle spit up gravel as they fought their way up the twisting mountain road. Up ahead, the lodge awaited. Despite my beautiful surroundings, the sight of the property made the hairs on my neck stand up. My tattoos twitched, sensing the dark magic concentrated at the peak of the mountain.

I was about to enter the lion's den. I knew a direct assault would end in failure. The various wards and magical defenses would stop me cold. Stealth was required for this operation. My magical tattoos started to burn, so I pulled my bike to the side of the road and hid behind a copse of trees and thick undergrowth.

And waited.

About ten minutes passed before another car appeared on the mountain road. The blue Jaguar could only be headed for the lodge. My lips turned upward in a satisfied smile. This was my ticket into the compound. I emerged from the shrubbery, and the Jaguar screeched to a tire-burning halt. I waved at the driver, a mid-thirties male who stared at me with saucer eyes.

As I approached, I stealthily caught my reflection in

the rear-view mirror, and his reaction started to make more sense. A stunning blonde in a skimpy red dress was staring back at me. Whoa! I had counted on my magical trench coat to cook up some effective disguise, and it had come through with flying colors. I was secure enough in my masculinity not to completely freak out over my magical sex change, knowing it was an illusion.

Or so I hoped.

The driver rolled down his window and regarded me with hungry eyes. Good. The fact that I was dealing with an occultist creep would make the next part a lot easier.

"Are you okay, ma'am? Did your bike break down?"

Another quick glance in the man's rear-view mirror revealed that the *Nighthawk* now looked like a red moped. Nice touch.

I tried batting my eyes at him. "I'm so sorry, I tried calling AAA but I'm not getting a signal up here? My provider sucks. I thought you might have better luck?"

The driver shook his head. "Cell phones don't work up here. Were you headed up to the retreat? They have a landline you can use. Just get in, and I'll hook you up."

I feigned slight hesitation, making sure I didn't seem too eager. I didn't want the driver to get suspicious.

"Come on, I don't bite."

*I do, buddy.* I smiled in what I hoped was a charming, shy way.

Still pretending to be wary of getting in a car with a

stranger, I slipped into the Jaguar and got comfortable in the passenger seat.

Now that I was inside, it was time to change my look.

I visualized what I wanted to look like, peered up at the rearview mirror to make sure it had worked, and saw the Jaguar's driver staring back at me. Shocked surprise rippled over the real man's features, but it was too late. My fist snapped out, closed around the man's throat, and started squeezing. Within seconds I had choked off the oxygen supply to his brain sufficiently enough for him to pass out and slump over the steering wheel.

I drew a square into the air, and his form blinked out of existence. A muffled thump emanated from the trunk. I was still learning the teleportation spell, and my range was a joke, but it was enough to remove the unconscious bastard from the car and let me take his place behind the wheel of the Jaguar.

I started the engine and made my way up to the sprawling estate. As the wrought-iron gate came into view, doubt crept into my thoughts. Did these freaks have some sort of secret code or handshake? As soon as I passed the security cams mounted near the entrance, the gate swung open.

I pulled into the lush property and parked in an area filled with Teslas, Mercedes, and BMWs. Octurna wasn't kidding when she said this organization made it a point to recruit powerful influencers. Judging by the luxury cars, this place had drawn the interest of its fair share of Hollywood shakers and makers. The idea that black magic might be encoded in my favorite popcorn flick or video game sent a shiver down my spine.

Giving myself an internal push, I silenced my whirling thoughts. *Concentrate on the mission, filter out the chatter.*

Calmed by this clarity of purpose, I parked my newly acquired Jaguar and got out. A few other people were walking up to the impressive property, and I fell in step with them. No one looked at each other or exchanged greetings. Everyone seemed to be in their own world. Good. I had not been looking forward to making small talk with the other attendees and blowing my cover in the process.

I trailed the group into the house, my muscles tense, eyes alert.

*What other security measures should I be worried about?* I mentally asked Octurna.

*"Look at the roof."*

The sorceresses' voice sounded distant and staticky. Our communication was breaking up. It must have been the mansion's magical defense system messing with our telepathic link.

I turned my focus to the mansion's rooftop. I didn't know exactly what I was looking for. Maybe more security cams or some other electronic security feature? I didn't spot anything out of the ordinary.

*"Look closer. Tap into your magic."*

Easier said than done. I was still getting the hang of all this combat magic stuff.

My eyes swept the rooftops again. I took note of the stone gargoyles, and then one of the winged rock statues began to stir. A subtle but unmistakable sign of preternatural life. My chest tightened and the hairs on my neck stood up. The creatures were alive, hiding among the statues, perfectly blending with their stone cousins. A quick glance revealed two more live gargoyles among the grotesques. I saw a flicker of red in the creatures' eyes, almost as if they could sense they were being observed.

I averted my gaze and prayed my curiosity hadn't blown my cover. Gargoyle security! What would these crazy mages think of next? Perched high above, able to see who was coming and going...had I been made?

*"I doubt it. Your magical disguise is strong enough to trick these simple creatures."*

It required all my will power not to steal another look at the roof. Maybe this wasn't such a good idea after all.

*"The Shadow Cabal has become complacent and lazy. For over a century, no one has dared to stand up against them. In the age of science, no one pays attention to magic. And that's how they like it. They feel safe and untouchable. That will change tonight. Tonight, we remind them that the past isn't dead yet."*

Octurna's speech boosted my confidence. The element

of surprise was in our favor. But I would have to make this first attack count.

I followed the crowd into the mansion and struggled to maintain my poker face as I took in the vulgar display of wealth and luxury. The views were as spectacular up here as I had hoped. A giant, seventy-five-foot infinity pool promised relief from the heat just beyond the massive bank of windows. The sun was setting, turning the sky blood red and bathing the guest's faces crimson, giving them an inhuman, almost demonic quality.

My boots clicked like a metronome against the marble floor as I explored the elaborate foyer. I entered a large hall split by a curving staircase. The chateau's exterior had been a perfect fusion of modern and classical architecture, and the same design aesthetic extended to the inside of the property. Sleek glass windows contrasted with dry-aged oak floors, handmade art fused with custom furnishings, stylish though a bit excessive. An octagonal marble bar dominated the reception area and seemed to offer up every brand of alcohol your liver could desire.

Dracula's castle it wasn't.

Or at least not yet. My eyes widened slightly I shuffled forward with a handful of folks into the next chamber, where people were undressing and slipping into hooded purple robes the host had generously provided.

I hesitated, unsure what my next move should be. The magical crystal ball inside my coat seemed to weigh a thousand pounds. Rivulets of sweat ran down the sides of my face. I had hoped the sorceress would guide me, but no such luck. I couldn't tell if she was ignoring me on purpose or if the mansion's wards hard blocked our telepathic link.

So how to proceed? The question now was one of timing. When and where to shatter the magical bomb and release its destructive power. I figured my best bet was to head to the center of the property to assure the maximum destruction. Judging by the singular focus of the robed guests, I figured they were about to attend a ceremony of some sort. Should I follow them and plant the bomb at their gathering place. That felt like a plan I could live with.

Mind made up, I slipped into one of the robes, unwilling to stick out from this eerily silent crowd. Hey, some folks think of the Marine Corps as a cult, and maybe they have a point but it was *my cult*, and you couldn't just join it, you had to earn your place in it.

My thoughts were going a bit crazy as I threw the hood over my head and continued to follow the purple mob down an adjoining hallway. For a change, I wished Octurna would speak up in my mind and let me know I wasn't flying solo here, but she remained silent.

I clenched my jaw and tried to keep my cool as I trailed the robed procession down a white corridor. A quick glance up ahead showed me that our group was marching toward a large oil painting. The artwork showed a three-dimensional view of a medieval stone corridor with the requisite whirling torches set in iron grips. Events took an even weirder turn when the first robed visitors stepped into the painting and advanced further down the stone hallway, the burning torches painting their purple robes as they became a part of the artwork.

This was more than just a painting. We were marching right toward a magical portal of some kind Who knew where it would lead us and how its magic might affect my disguise.

I had to turn back. Find some chamber in the mansion and shatter the crystal.

These thoughts were racing my mind when I heard the scream. It belonged to a woman, a shriek of unbridled terror which rattled me to the core. And it had emanated from the oil painting. Dammit! Someone was in trouble.

Could I just ignore the pitiful cry for help? More importantly, if I detonated the magical bomb, would I doom the screamer to a fiery death?

Pressed along by the robed crowd behind me, I had little choice. My lips pressed into a thin line as the surface of the painting shimmered and gave way. My next step struck rough stone instead of polished tile. I looked back and saw that the mansion's modern hallway had become an oil painting inside the medieval structure.

A chill trickled down the base of my spine. I was looking at a painting within a painting.

Another scream rang through the stone corridor,

confirming that I was doing the right thing. Someone was in danger. Mortal danger, judging by the shrill panic in the woman's voice.

I continued to follow the procession of purple robes down the shadowy passageway, wishing they would hurry the hell up. The crystal ball inside my trench coat seemed to weigh a thousand pounds.

We all entered a circular stone observation area that overlooked a rough-hewn stone pit. Torches provided ample illumination, and I spotted a terrified figure thirty feet below. My eyes widened, and I felt rage bubbling up my throat. The brunette was practically naked, her skirt and blouse shredded, her hair wild and unkempt, eyes squirming with fear as she peered up at the purple-robed mob. She tugged on her restraints and snarled a curse. Even though she must've gone through God knows what torture, she hadn't given up. Despite her fear, I saw something else in those eyes. Strength. Courage. Defiance.

A familiar voice thrust me out of my thoughts. It belonged to Professor Brogan.

"Welcome, my brothers and sisters. I thank you for gracing us with your presence tonight. Today, we have something special planned. Only recently did we learn that someone tried to infiltrate our organization…"

Stunned gasps and moans of surprise rang through the crowd.

For a split second, my hand went for my handgun,

expecting to be outed in front of this crowd. But Brogan was apparently referring to the woman in the bone-covered pit.

"Look at her. Using beauty and charm to gain access to our lodge. A reporter chasing a story, hoping to shed light on what happens at our meetings. A fool who is about to pay the ultimate price for her curiosity."

Brogan turned his attention to the nearly naked woman in the pit.

"You've come here, your heart full of deceit, your soul hungry for answers."

"Let me go!" Her voice was hoarse from exhaustion, and I felt my heart going out to her. "Damn it, I won't tell anyone what I saw. Just let me out of here!"

Brogan smiled in response to the woman's words. "Oh, I know you won't. Not after tonight."

I gritted my teeth. What were these freaks planning? I received my answer a second later as the giant gate rumbled open inside the pit, and a nightmarish shadow fell over the bone-covered grounds. The reporter's courage crumpled, and she let out another piercing scream.

I swallowed hard. The real horror show was about to begin.

## 13

Mighty footsteps shook the pit, and the violent vibrations rattled the observation deck. My pulse quickened, and I swore softly.

The massive beast emerging from the gate was humanoid and about ten feet tall, albino-skinned with bulging muscles. Its powerful shoulders were twice the size of a man, its features pallid and pitted with two ugly red wounds for eyes. Webs of blue and green arteries and veins formed networks under the transparent, ghostlike skin, and repulsive pink warts covered much of its torso like a patch of mushrooms. Horns of varying sizes, too many to count, pockmarked the thing's otherwise bald scalp.

Being somewhat new to this monster fighting business, I had no idea what sort of nightmare creature I was looking at. All I knew was that it looked dangerous and pissed and was one ugly fucker.

It was a safe bet to say that the remaining lifespan of the screaming woman could be measured in heartbeats at this point. As the monster lumbered toward her, I noticed its dangling sex stiffening between its legs. The creature had something far worse in store for the reporter than a mauling.

The purple-robed crowd of cabalists cheered with excitement, eager for the show to begin. Sick fucks! Fury sizzled up my throat, and my heart turned icy with anger. These soulless, decadent bastards wanted to be entertained, and I decided to deliver a performance they wouldn't so soon forget.

The time had come to act.

So far, I had been a silent observer in the unfolding drama. Honestly, I had hoped to plant my magical bomb and steal off into the night. That was no longer an option. There was no way I could let this poor woman meet her terrible fate in the pit below.

Unwilling to sit this one out on the sidelines any longer, I freed myself from the purple robe in one fluid motion, and shouldered my magically charged submachine gun. I leveled the weapon and unloaded a full magazine into the monster.

The staccato bursts of furious gunfire rattled the stone veranda overlooking the pit, and the cabalists standing near me recoiled in shocked surprise. My bullets tore deep gashes into the monster's fish-belly flesh and spattered its swollen muscles with dripping gore.

Magazine spent, I reloaded like a machine and pumped a few quick shots into the purple group of cabalists before they did something stupid like trying to rush me. As the robed freaks backed away from the traitor in their midst, I swiveled toward the beast in the medieval arena below and found the giant staring back at me. Glowing red eyes bored into my soul with murderous hunger. Bloody graffiti covered the beast's muscular chest, and it looked more pissed off than hurt.

I was still considering my next move when the pink warts on the creature's upper body opened like the petals of some mutated flower, and a collection of tentacles exploded from the unsightly growths.

One of the thrashing appendages snapped around my torso like the lasso of some overeager cowboy and pulled me to the edge of the stone catwalk. The creature's intent was clear—it was hoping to pull me into its bone-littered playpen.

*Not so fast, buddy.*

I nimbly whipped out one of the silver daggers from my bandolier and sliced the undulating limb apart. The severed piece of tentacle hugging my waist stiffened and dropped to the ground while the other half gushed red and withdrew into the pink boil from which it had sprung.

Thankfully, I had skipped the hors d'oeuvres on the way in and didn't have to worry about spray-painting the bleachers with the contents of my stomach. That shit was *nasty*.

The creature howled with agony and frustration. Before I could launch into a victory dance, two more tentacles found me, lashed around my throat and wrist, and with a vicious yank, whisked me into the pit.

That's when my training kicked in.

As the ground came rushing up, I instinctively drew a quick triangle in the air with my free left hand. Reality warped and sizzled, and a protective energy shield formed around me. Instead of being reduced to a broken pile of bones, I landed on a cushion of magical energy.

A roar cut through the arena as the serpentine limbs released me. I glared at the beast as it howled with pain and fury, its gaping mouth splitting the gargantuan head in two. Gleaming teeth emerged from its gums like claws unsheathed from a cat's paw.

One more tentacle unfurled toward me, and this one sported a six-inch curved stinger. I tried to sidestep the incoming projectile, but my timing was slightly off, and the stinger tore into my chest like an oversized fish-hook. I gasped, biting back a scream as blood erupted from my punctured chest and coated my skin-tight black combat suit.

I reflexively snatched the flailing tentacle. The long

sparring sessions with the golem sisters were paying off. Nerve endings exploded in my injured side, and my legs grew wobbly, but I steadfastly refused to let go of the monster's twitching feeler. Tapping into every available reservoir of strength, I jerked the stinger out of my shoulder. Pain twisted my lips but, I didn't release the tentacle. Instead, I violently pulled on it.

Time to reel in my catch.

The beast drunkenly trundled toward me and opened its massive jaws, intent on biting off my head, T-Rex style.

As its shadow swept over me, my gauntlet sprouted twin blades. The sound of the knives exploding from the steel glove was music to my ears. With a ferocious snarl, I lashed out. The blades found the creature's dangling manhood and severed it from his bulging body in a spray of scarlet.

I've seen some gruesome shit over the years. Two wars had taught me what steel and fire can do to the human body. But seeing a elephant trunk-sized, red-veined albino monster dick soaring through a medieval arena was a new one even for me.

For an eternal moment, the giant glowered at me in shock, unable to process what had happened to the favorite part of his anatomy. And then all hell broke loose as the beast went ape shit. I couldn't blame the creature.

Its pitiful wails echoed through the arena. Didn't matter if you were a man or a monster, that was about the worst thing that could happen to a member of the male species. Knowing what this bastard had planned to do to the captive reporter, I didn't feel too sorry for him.

I turned away from the screaming mountain of heaving muscle and spun toward the woman. She stared at me like a child greeting the first morning light after a long night of nightmares.

"Are you alright?" I asked lamely. Of course she wasn't.

The ground shook, and a quick glance told me the castrated monster was ready to smash us both into a bloody pulp despite the gushing injury between its legs.

"Give me your gun!" the reporter said, snapping out of her daze. I was almost afraid to hand her the firearm, uncertain what she might so. But something about the way she eyed me swept my hesitation aside. The strength I had spotted earlier had edged back into her gaze.

"Please," she pleaded, desperation in her voice. She wanted this. *Needed it.*

I handed her the sidearm, grip first. She released the safety and leveled it at the wailing beast. Without a trace of hesitation, she unloaded a full magazine into the creature's open mouth. A hail of silver bullets found the soft tissue, and the monster's enormous head snapped back, the sound of gunfire strangling its dying bellows.

The damsel in distress had expertly nailed the head shot.

The giant toppled stiffly like a felled tree, its crumpling

body headed straight for us. Before tons of monster flesh could bury us, I grabbed the woman's hand and dragged her out of the path of the crashing giant. The beast slammed into the ground with devastating force, the impact of its lifeless body rattling the pit.

With a final grotesque gurgle, it exited from this world. The thing's inhuman death rattle sending a shiver up my spine. And then it made no sound at all, bloody froth bubbling from its bullet-perforated lips. I wasn't about to take the beast's pulse, but I was pretty sure the reporter's bullets had finished it off.

Thick blood seeped into dusty ground, and I felt the power surging within me. Even though I technically hadn't delivered the death blow, the tattoos on my body were absorbing the creature's infernal energy. But if Octurna expected me to bring her the giant's skull, she had another thing coming.

I traded a quick glance with the reporter, impressed. She had handled my sidearm like a pro, and I suspected this wasn't the first time she'd fired a weapon.

"Who the hell are you?" someone called out.

The voice reverberated through the pit. For a moment, I had been so distracted by both Beauty and the Beast that I'd forgotten about our audience of blood-thirsty cabalists. They peered down at us in hushed silence, clearly stunned that I had defeated their monstrous pet. I scanned the ring of purple and found the speaker. It was none other than

Professor Brogan. Judging by the way he carried himself, he was the head honcho in this lodge.

Our eyes met, and we stared at each other for a beat.

"We will know soon enough," Brogan said. "Get the intruder!"

Brogan waved his hands, drawing circles in the air, indicating he was about to cast a spell. I had used up my shield during my fall, so there was nothing I could do but take a wait-and-see approach at this point. I steeled myself for the worst. Luckily, I didn't turn into a frog or a puddle of ectoplasmic goo. I saw a ripple of green energy engulf the throng of robed cabalists. The crowd jumped to their feet, and one by one, they dove with inhuman athletic grace into the thirty-foot-deep pit, robes billowing around them, murder in their eyes. For a surreal moment, I recognized some of the cabalists. One was a classic pop star from the eighties, another was an up-and-coming movie actor.

And then my celebrity spotting gave away to the more pressing need for survival.

We had to escape this death trap. Now!

Lightning fast, I popped another magazine into my submachine gun. I tossed a 9mm mag at the battered woman next to me. We both reloaded at the same time and depressed the triggers of our weapons. Our guns roared, and bullets whipped into the mass of robed fanatics.

I dashed toward the slain beast and swiftly climbed its

corpse until I stood on its bloody shoulders. I had acquired the high ground. From this elevated angle, I unleashed renewed bursts at the mob threatening to encircle us.

Another phalanx of cabalists went down, purple robes turning red, but for every cabalist who fell in battle, two new enemies took their place. More and more of them kept dropping into the pit, eyes possessed, moving with an inhuman grace as if they were extras in some sick remake of *The Matrix*.

Three of the robed assailants landed on me. The impact sent me flying. In a flailing tangle of limbs, the three cabalists and I rolled down the dead giant's corpse and hit the dusty pit. I was still getting my bearings when four more cabalists attacked. I had not been a slouch in the fighting department even before loading up on dragon blood, but these punches hurt. The fists raining down on me glowed with green light. Somehow, Brogan had transferred his own burgeoning magical powers to the crowd and turned them each into a bunch of murderous badasses.

I activated my gauntlet and went to town. The twin blades sliced through the robes and found the flesh underneath. My knives tore through one man's chest and burst through his back, slick with gore.

I withdrew the two blades with a wet splat only to cleave the next cabalist's face in half. He went down in a spray of red, looking like a grizzly bear had mistaken his face for a honeypot. A third assailant closed in, unfazed by the fate of its fallen brothers.

Brogan's magic hadn't just given these cultists super-strength. It had transformed everyone into an irrational berserker. They reminded me of people high on PCP, uncaring of their own safety.

So far, I had managed to stand my ground, but ultimately their sheer numbers would overwhelm me. I had to get out of this pit. Picking off these cabalists one by one was a fool's errand. Much better to let my magical bomb do the dirty work. But I couldn't detonate the bomb while still in the pit. See my problem?

I never meant this to be a suicide mission. Fortunately, my whole body surged with the energy I'd sapped from the dead monster. And my newfound power inspired an idea. Could I teleport myself and the reporter through space and materialize on the stone veranda above the pit? In the past, my range for the spell had only been a few feet. I wasn't sure we'd make it. But it was worth a try. The power rippling through my tattoos was immense, and it gave me the confidence to try the impossible.

My gaze turned upward, and I fixed on the stone high above. Most of the cabalists had jumped into the pit except for Brogan and a few others I guessed were his top men. The good professor was busy powering his cabalist strike force.

*Now or never, Night.*

I snatched the reporter's hand, said a quick prayer, and closed my eyes. I could hear the robed throng closing in on us, their feet slapping against the pit's stone floor. Their rage and hatred and killer instinct seemed to cloud the air. It was hard to concentrate, but I couldn't let the dire nature of our situation get in the way of the spell I was about to cast. I had to turn inward, shut it all out, and tap into my new abilities.

I had to embrace who I was—the Night Slayer.

For a split second, nothing happened. And then reality shimmered and warped. Both the pit and the incoming crowd of cabalists phased out of existence in a flash of blinding energy.

## 14

The world of the pit with its crowd of crazed cabalists vanished, replaced with the perfect darkness of the void. All sounds drained from the world. I felt at peace with myself and the universe. I was physically travelling through space, carried along by an invisible current.

But I wasn't alone in this dark yet comfortable place.

I stole a glance to my right, and I saw the reporter, her eyes wide with wonder. Despite the surreal quality of the experience, we felt no fear.

The brief moment of tranquility came to an abrupt end as light flooded the darkness. Reality intruded on the peaceful blackness, and we found ourselves on the circular observation platform where I had caught my first glimpse of the woman now standing by my side.

I was able to look down into the pit and saw the mass

of purple-clad cabalists descending on a ghostlike shadow image of us. The mob hesitated, unsure what had happened. They would figure it out soon enough. We had traveled about thirty feet through space. We were not in the clear just yet, but fortunately only a couple of cabalists blocked the passageway leading back to the painting portal.

The reporter fell in step with me as I ran down the passageway. I didn't dare steal a glance back at Brogan. Last I checked, the head mage was a tad distracted with his efforts as a magical puppeteer. He was the battery powering this insanity, and hopefully his own spell had drained him sufficiently so that I wouldn't have to worry about any nasty magical surprises.

Guns blazing, we blasted our way through the few remaining cabalists. I tossed one robed enemy over the stone railing into the pit thirty feet below. He screamed all the way to the bottom until the sickening crunch of his spine snapping silenced him. The head of another cabalist vanished in a puff of crimson mist. I was really starting to like this girl.

We barreled into the medieval passageway and surged toward the magical painting-portal located at the far end. My face set in a determined mask, I flung myself through the shimmering oil painting, my left hand tight around the reporter's wrist. Energy crackled around us, and then we were back inside the sleek Malibu chateau. Two cabalists milling in the hallway regarded us with big eyes. Before either one of them could make a peep, they both sprouted cyclopean third eyes and collapsed in string-cut sprawls, the white marble floors turning red.

I extricated the blue shimmering crystal ball from my coat and felt the reporter's questioning gaze on me. There was no time to explain. The answers to her questions would have to wait until later. I silently prayed that I had enough magical juice left to shatter the orb. The teleportation spell had taken a lot out of me, and my whole body ached. My chest throbbed crazily, waves of pain spiking my body.

*Just hang in there a bit longer, buddy,* I told myself.

Fortunately, the next step didn't require an enormous amount of power. Within seconds of focusing my magic on the ball, cracks started to form over its surface. A heartbeat later, the crystal orb shattered into a thousand pieces. Tendrils of blood-red mist began to spread through the beautiful yet sterile white hallways of the chateau.

Icy fear speared through me as I watched the fog spread. Every hair on my body stood on end, sensing the destructive power of those swirling clouds of red.

Determined to put some distance between us and the scarlet mist before it reached its deadly potential, I swiftly crossed the great hall. The reporter followed at a brisk trot. The remaining guests cleared a path for us as we beelined toward the exit. I guess my black combat suit and the reporter's shredded outfit set us apart from the purple robe crowd. Anyone foolish enough to confront us backed off the instant they spotted my glowing green submachine gun and blood-spattered clothing.

*That's right, guys, you don't want to fuck with us.*

One doorman decided to get frisky and trained his sidearm on my center mass. I rewarded his efforts with two quick shots to the head, spraying a nearby Greek statue with his chunky brain matter. I sent a piercing glare in the direction of the second doorman, who wisely dropped his pistol and shuffled aside. We brushed past him, guns leveled, ready to kill at the slightest provocation.

And then we were outside the mansion.

Running for our lives.

Screams erupted in the chateau behind us, and this time I hazarded a quick backward glance. The magical red mist had thickened. It now obscured the oblong windows of the mansion. A shadow appeared in one of the windows —the glass shattered, and a cabalist exploded from within. Clouds of swirling red energy covered him. With horror, I saw the mist literally strip the flesh off his body. A second later, it consumed the dead man's bones.

Suddenly, I was glad that Octurna hadn't shared the details of her magical bomb with me.

I forced myself to look away from the dissolving corpse and focused on the luxury cars parked in front of me. I spotted the blue Jaguar I'd acquired earlier and made a go for the vehicle. As I approached, I took note of the loud pounding noise coming from inside the vehicle's trunk. The driver I'd knocked out was awake.

I popped the trunk. The cabalist jumped out, armed with a knife which he must have kept hidden in the trunk. The blade aimed at the reporter.

Before he could drive the knife into her, I drilled the cabalist in the forehead. I wasn't taking any prisoners today. Thinking back to my dying team members melted away all traces of hesitation. This was war. And the Shadow Cabal was the enemy.

The reporter stared at me, clearly shocked by my capacity for violence but also grateful. I had saved her a second time.

I flung the passenger door open. "Get in the car!"

She did as she was told.

I slipped behind the steering wheel, cranked the engine, and stole another glance into the rear-view mirror. The red mist had now fully enveloped the chateau, and the screams inside had died down. By now, the terrible fog must have destroyed all life within its walls. It seemed that it was turning its devastating energy against the structure itself. Terrible sounds of destruction filled the air as the foundation of the chateau cracked and shook, tendrils of red spinning faster and faster around the Malibu castle. The crimson force transformed into a fearsome tornado. Windows blew out, walls collapsed, the surrounding plant life wilted.

The mansion was being erased from reality.

I'd seen explosives in action too many times to count, witnessed smart bombs incinerate vehicles and buildings. This was even worse. Slower, more deliberate. As the mansion's foundation succumbed to the magical forces battering against it, a giant sinkhole opened up and swallowed the Malibu estate. Crimson light bled over the property, expanding rapidly like some hellish, all-devouring virus.

Octurna hadn't been joking when she urged me to go scorched earth on the place. At this rate, nothing much would remain of the Shadow Cabal's party pad. Talk about sending the bad guys a message they wouldn't be able to ignore.

As the mountain consumed what was left of the building, I saw movement on the disintegrating rooftops. Three winged shadows erupted into the air and emerged from the billowing cloud of red.

The three sentinel gargoyles. The winged bastards were zeroing in on the Jaguar.

Shit!

I floored the gas and blasted out of the property, the three pissed-off gargoyles in hot pursuit.

We shot down the winding mountain road, swathes of trees and thick undergrowth zooming past my field of vision. The waves of magical red light had turned night into day. It looked like a previously unknown volcano had erupted on top of the Malibu mountain.

The dragon blood had enhanced my senses, including my hearing and night vision. I could hear the wings of the beasts slicing the air, saw their muscular shapes cutting toward us in my rear-view mirror.

They had failed to spot me when I first infiltrated the Cabal lodge. Preventing my escape was their best shot at redemption. After battling the Hulk's repugnant cousin, three gargoyles didn't faze me. Or at least they didn't at first. As they drew closer, I began to understand that these nasty fuckers posed their own unique challenge.

I turned to the reporter, whose name I still didn't know, and said, "Think you can drive?"

She regarded me for a beat, studied the rear-view mirror and the incoming gargoyles, and then nodded. Our bodies brushed against each other as we switched seats while hurtling down the mountain road. I tried to be a gentleman about the whole thing but couldn't help but notice that my passenger was practically naked. Fortunately, the shrieking gargoyles were keeping my mind out of the gutter. Mostly.

The reporter grabbed the wheel and expertly navigated the vehicle down the steep road.

"So you can shoot guns and drive like a stuntwoman," I said. "Anything else you can do?"

She flashed me a quick grin, and I knew I could trust her.

Reassured by this exchange, I popped the sunroof open and stuck my head out. Within seconds, I shouldered my machine pistol and tried to get a bead on our three aerial pursuers as the Jaguar swerved down the twisting road. The reporter took a curve too fast, and I nearly fell out. My wound was burning as if someone had poured sizzling hot oil on it. A dull ache gnawed at my brain. So much for the regenerative abilities of my dragon blood.

I clenched my jaw, sighted my submachine gun on the lead gargoyle sweeping in for the kill, and squeezed the trigger. Gunfire shredded the air, and silver bullets peppered the creature's head, chest, and wings. The gargoyle's aerial maneuver turned into a crash landing as it slammed with ferocious speed into the mountain road. The impact rattled my teeth and shook the car.

No time to celebrate my victory. I needed to focus on the two remaining gargoyles.

As I reloaded my weapon, the second gargoyle landed on the trunk of the car with a loud thump. The vehicle swerved for a moment, and I feared the reporter might lose control. Fortunately, the car straightened out, and I let out a sigh of relief despite the gargoyle now eyeing me with lethal intent.

*Good Girl*, I thought.

The beast roared at me, wings flailing while its claws

remained buried in steel. Sharp teeth tore towards me, and I returned the greeting with the twin knives of my gauntlet. Moonlight glinted on the two blades as they ripped through the winged beast's throat and exploded from the back of his neck in a spray of black blood. I savagely twisted my wrist, and the creature detached from the vehicle, vanishing to the side of the road in a convulsing heap of flailing wings.

Two down, one to go. So where was the third bastard?

I scanned the air and spotted the remaining creature trailing us from high above. Apparently, the last gargoyle was trying to learn from the mistakes of his fallen brothers. Instead of dive-bombing me, it kept its distance, zigzagging back and forth, determined to not make for an easy target.

I blocked out the pulsing pain in my shoulder and tried to get a lock on the gargoyle. But it moved faster than one would expect for a creature its size. And then it soared past us overhead, pulled in front of the rapidly descending Jaguar, and dove toward the windshield.

The creature's strategy was clear. Having decided that I was too dangerous, it was making a go for the driver.

A deafening boom tore through the night as gunfire erupted from the windshield. Silver bullets slammed into the incoming beast, and I wasn't the one who'd pulled the trigger. The reporter had emptied her firearm with one hand while driving with the other, but the slick gambit came at a price. She now fought the Jaguar into a screaming turn and side-swiped grass and shrubbery growing along the side of the roadway.

The maneuver almost sent me flying again, but with lightning speed, I drove my two blades into the roof of the car, anchoring myself in place. With the other hand, I drilled a few more bullets into the downed gargoyle, taking advantage of the easy target it made on the side of the road.

For a moment, I just sucked in the sweet night air, with its faint hint of the nearby ocean, and allowed the waves of adrenaline to subside.

We did it. We had blown up the lodge and managed to escape in one piece. There was the matter of my nasty shoulder injury, but I had a feeling Octurna might be able to help me out on that front—or so I hoped.

As my racing pulse settled, I slipped back into the car and traded a quick glance with the reporter. She sported a thousand-yard stare and barely acknowledge my presence. One hand white-knuckled the steering wheel while the other clutched the smoking handgun. She was a hell of a woman. Call me impressed.

The reporter's distant gaze cleared, feeling my attention on her. A hint of a smile curled her lips as she came back to the present moment. I returned the smile.

*"Well done, slayer."*

I hated to admit, but I was glad to hear Octurna in my

head again after the long silence. *Thanks, boss,* I communicated silently.

"*I see you made a new friend,*" she continued. Was there a note of jealousy in Octurna's voice? Then her tone softened. "*You're injured...*"

*Yeah, some giant drilled me with his stinger.*

"*Describe the creature.*"

*Big. Pale. Muscular. Ugly as fuck. With tentacles...*

"*Sounds like you fought a Nockmar... You're lucky to be alive. You must immediately return to the Sanctuary. I will try to materialize the fortress.*"

*What about the Nighthawk?* I mentally asked. Hey, I'd gotten attached to my new set of wheels.

"*Don't worry about it for the moment.*"

I sensed the reporter studying my expression, almost like she could sense the inner dialogue I was having with Octurna.

*Tell me what to do,* I thought.

"*I will materialize at the end of the...*"

Octurna's voice broke off, grew faint. What was happening? My mind turned blank as a migraine sprouted to life behind my eyeballs. I inhaled sharply. My vision swam and then the darkness came crashing down on me.

The blood loss had finally caught up with me. The last thing I remember hearing was the reporter's voice as she asked if I was okay.

*Not even close, lady.*

## 15

I came to in a murky haze. Disorientation greeted me. Where the hell was I?

I took in the details of my unfamiliar surroundings. I was on a soft bed inside a sparsely decorated bedroom. Considering that I neither found myself in a hospital or back in the Sanctuary, I probably had to be in the reporter's home. I was shirtless, and a thick bandage covered my shoulder injury. The throbbing had subsided somewhat, suggesting that the reporter had cleaned the wound and applied a pretty good field dressing. I heard the sound of running water coming from the adjacent room. Someone was taking a shower.

My gaze traveled to a nearby dresser, drawn to a collection of framed pictures that confirmed that I was in the reporter's apartment. I had saved her, and she was returning the favor. I wondered why she hadn't taken me to a hospital. Maybe my wound and get-up would have raised too many questions. And I bet she had some questions of her own.

Studying the pictures proved educational. It showed the lovely journalist in various cities across the globe. In one shot, she posed with Iraqi special forces; in another she was covering the devastation in Puerto Rico in the wake of last year's hurricane. The girl had gotten around. And wasn't afraid to risk her life in the pursuit of a good story. My respect for her continued to grow.

I tried to climb out of bed, but the sharp jolt in my chest painfully reminded me I wasn't in the clear yet. I exhaled sharply, bit my tongue, and tried it again. I gasped as I stood up and limped toward the nearest window. A quick glimpse outside revealed Wilshire and Lincoln Boulevards as my cross streets. I was in a high-rise apartment building located in Santa Monica, eight stories above the glittering cars on the streets below. It was still dark outside, and judging by the lively traffic, it couldn't be past midnight yet, suggesting I hadn't been out that long.

Still feeling weak, I stumbled back to the bed and laid down again. I knew where I was now.

The shoulder wasn't throbbing, but weirdly enough, the discomfort had traveled inside my chest and stomach. I remembered the urgency in Octurna's voice when I had described the monster who attacked me. Had that thing poisoned me? I had to get back to the Sanctuary.

Easier said than done. I attempted to reach out to the sorceress, but my words fell on deaf ears. And then I remembered the magical motorcycle I had left in Malibu. Not exactly the type of equipment you wanted to leave behind. I felt like a teenager who had taken his dad's expensive car out for a joyride and failed to return it. Octurna wouldn't be pleased. She'd be even less pleased if I let myself die in Santa Monica.

I was still going over my options when the shower turned off. I waited for a minute. The door opened, and the reporter emerged from the bathroom. She was wearing a robe, her damp mane of auburn blonde hair clinging to her face. Standing there in her light blue bathrobe, skin glistening, she looked even more stunning than I would have guessed. This woman had an earthy, untamed quality about her—petite, athletic and less voluptuous than Octurna but equally tantalizing. Her eyes met my admiring gaze and held it, our chemistry palpable.

She slipped beside me into bed, still wrapped in her bathrobe.

"How are you feeling?"

"Like I went head-to-head with a T-Rex."

She smiled softly. "Don't tell me you've done that before?"

"Not yet," I chuckled.

"Thank you for saving me," she said, her voice emotional.

She touched my hand. I leaned forward, almost kissing her. Her freshly washed hair smelled like citrus. Clean and wholesome, like sunshine. And then our arms and legs instinctively wrapped around each other, both of us seeking solace and comfort in the other's warmth. It felt both natural and necessary after the terrors of the Cabal lodge. This wasn't some cheesy movie love scene; we were both too emotionally and physically drained for heated passion. No, we clung to each other inside our shared warmth, a celebration of being alive and having overcome great horrors as we unwound our taut nerves. Sobbing softly against my chest, she continued to whisper the same two words into my ears, her breath on my skin.

*"Thank you, thank you."*

We stayed like this for who knows long, more in need of closeness and connection than physical release.

"What's your name?" I asked, my fingers brushing through her wet hair.

"Keira."

"Nice to meet you, Keira. I'm Jason."

"You look familiar. Have we met before?"

I thought about this for a second. As a SWAT commander, I had given my share of news interviews over the last few years but didn't want to go into my full background at the moment. I decided to steer the conversation in a new direction.

I nodded at the photographs. "I see you get around."

"I like to keep busy," she said with a smile.

"Some nice moves back at the mansion. Who taught you how to shoot guns and drive like that?"

Her lips stretched into a sexy grin. It was nice to see her amused.

"My dad. He was a Navy SEAL who wanted a son."

"I bet he's proud of his daughter."

She gave me a ragged smile. "All my friends growing up were taking ballet while I was shooting and practicing martial arts with my dad."

Encouraged by the strength in Keira's voice, I shifted to a more painful subject. "How long did they keep you at the mansion?"

"Five long days," Keira said with a heavy voice.

"You were doing a story on the...the group that meets there?"

"The Order of New Magic. We had heard rumors of a new cult that was gaining popularity and attracting a lot of Hollywood types. I was supposed to infiltrate the organization and do an exposé for the Times. My cover was solid, and I had gained the trust of a few of the Order's members. I thought I was getting somewhere when they invited me to the Malibu mansion. I never expected..."

She broke off, the memories threatening to overwhelm her. She didn't need to say more. Best not to dwell on the fate that had awaited her in the pit.

"It's okay," I said. "You're safe now."

"The things I saw you do in the mansion... Who are you?"

"A friend."

She chuckled warmly and pressed deeper into my body. "I know that. But how...where did you come from? Your weapons, the things you did with your hands... You went all Harry Potter meets the Punisher on those guys..."

"Are you fishing for a story?" I said, trying to make a joke.

Keira flashed me a ragged smile. "You think anyone would print a story like this? I need to understand what's going on here if I ever want to catch a good night's sleep again."

"This madness is new to me too," I finally said. "What I can tell you is that monsters and magic are real. Bad people live in the shadows of our world, and I'm going to stop them."

The determination in my voice surprised me. I remembered my hesitation after I destroyed the succubus, the doubts about my role in all of this. My experience at the lodge had fundamentally changed my outlook. Octurna had told me this was my fight as much as hers. At the time, those had just been words. Now they actually meant something. I was committed to this mission. No one else stood a chance against the Shadow Cabal. Even the best intelligence agencies in the world couldn't oppose an organization if they weren't even aware of their enemy's existence.

More importantly, what good were guns and special operatives against magic and supernatural monsters? Fire had to be fought with fire. Magic with magic.

Kiera traced a fingertip down my arm. "I couldn't help notice your tattoos. They feel warm to the touch."

*They are the source of my magic,* I thought but couldn't bring myself to say it. Within the medieval walls of Octurna's Sanctuary, the craziness of the last few weeks somehow all made sense. The setting had normalized the fantastic. Now, back in the real world, it all started to feel like a dream, some elaborate fantasy that wouldn't bear the critical scrutiny of reality.

"Who are you really, Jason?"

*The Night Slayer*, I wanted to say in my best Batman voice, but I felt ridiculous even thinking about it.

"I don't know where to start."

"Try the beginning."

I regarded this beautiful woman, saw the vulnerability beneath her strength, her desperate need to make sense of what happened to her. Keira deserved to hear the truth. Otherwise, she would drive herself mad. It might not happen the next day or even the next week, but as time went by, the questions would continue to gnaw at her brain until her mind wouldn't be able to take it anymore. Her sense of the world had been severely shattered. She needed me to pick up all the broken pieces and stick them back together in a way that would make sense to her. I didn't even know if I could explain this insanity to her satisfaction, but I had to try.

And so I did.

At first, the words came haltingly. My story started to flow as I found myself caught up in the events of the last month. I wisely skipped the dirty parts and concentrated on the critical details.

Keira relaxed as I spoke. As fantastical as it all sounded, my story added up, especially considering what she had witnessed with her own eyes. I didn't need to convince her that gargoyles and tentacle beasts and magic were all real. Once I wrapped my tale, I let out a long breath. As therapeutic as my story was for Keira, my retelling was also helping me put the last month in some sort of perspective and context. For a change, I was the one with the answers. Until this point, I hadn't realized how much I'd needed this, needed to see the fantastic reflected back to me in the eyes of a regular person. My crazy tale proved to both Keira and myself that we hadn't lost our minds.

She regarded me differently as her fingers trailed the lines of my tattoos. Her touch was electric, and my body stirred.

Our earlier embrace had awoken something in us both. Desire.

Emotional needs were giving way to physical ones.

I barely remembered opening her robe and slipping

out of my pants. Hungry lips and roaming hands explored each other. I stopped thinking about the pain in my chest and focused entirely on Keira now. Our lovemaking was intense and frantic, pent-up terror and anxiety desperate for a physical outlet. We both came at the same time, and our bodies shuddered and groaned with pleasure. Sweaty, limbs tangled, unwilling to let go.

We lay together for a few more minutes. It was Keira who ultimately broke the silence.

"I want to help you. Let me stand with you while you face these horrors."

"You don't have the training..."

"Neither did you, until a month ago..."

"That's different," I protested.

"How so? Besides, I wasn't saying I need a bunch of fancy weapons and spells. I can help in other ways."

I processed these words. To be honest, the reporter's willingness to confront the horrors impressed me. Most people would have retreated into a world of denial and tried to rationalize the impossible. Not this girl. Not Keira.

Octurna and I had become mankind's best chance against the darkness, but could the two of us defeat this enemy on our own? I doubted it. Now that the Shadow Cabal knew of our existence, they would come after us without mercy. We would need allies in the battles ahead. And I was beginning to believe that Keira could be one of them. Only one hurdle remained—what would the sorceress think of this idea?

*"Never wise for a man to make important decisions while in the arms of a new conquest."*

I almost jolted back from Keira, the sorceress' voice in my head catching me off guard. Talk about weird timing. How long had she been listening in on our intimate exchange? And had she watched us make love on one of her windows?

"Very funny," I said. Judging by Keira's searching expression, I realized I had spoken out loud.

*"Jason, you must immediately get back to the Sanctuary. The Cabal is tracking you..."*

She started to break up, the words becoming garbled and turning to gibberish in my head. Something was interfering with our telepathic link. There was only one thing it could be: black magic.

The Cabal was on my tail. How were they tracking me?

This question was still cycling through my mind when the tattoos on my body lit up with red energy.

Keira recoiled. "What's going on?"

My tats crackled with a surge of power. I jumped out of bed, nerves on edge, jaw clenched.

"Get dressed! We have to get out of here!"

I didn't have to repeat myself. The alarm in my voice and fear in my wild gaze told its own story.

I had just finished putting on my pants when I spotted the shadow outside the window.

I froze for a beat, eyes fixed on the bizarre sight that now confronted me. Hovering behind the pane of glass, floating eight stories in midair as if auditioning for a starring role in a remake of *The Lost Boys*, was Professor Brogan. Had he been floating outside the window while I told my story to Keira—while we sought and found peace and comfort in each other's arms? No, my tattoos would have warned me.

I wondered how he found us. More importantly, how had he survived the magical bomb? The reach of the explosive must've been limited to the mansion. The Cabal acolyte had remained safe within the pocket dimension of the oil painting.

Brogan's slate-gray eyes burned with an unholy fire, electricity running up his hand as he drew a circle in the air. I had become familiar with the gesture over the last few days.

The bastard was about to cast a spell.

## 16

I expected the window to shatter as a burst of incredible magical energy speared into Keira's apartment. What followed in the wake of Brogan's hand gesture was both less dramatic and even more mind-boggling. One moment I was staring into Brogan's eyes; the next, I was completely submerged underwater, struggling to breathe. With horror, I realized the entire apartment had filled with water, and I was looking out at a smiling Brogan like a fish trapped in an aquarium.

I swapped a quick glance with a terrified Keira. Brogan's magic obviously was far more advanced than my own, plus I was unarmed and wounded. Saying the odds weren't in our favor was putting it mildly.

I spun around in the freezing cold water and dove toward the floor where Keira had stashed my gear. A plan was forming in the back of my mind. Grab my weapons, snatch Keira, and make a go for the apartment's exit. We would run out of breath in seconds. My lungs were already screaming for precious air. Neither one of us had had a chance to take a deep breath before Brogan struck. I prayed that Brogan hadn't flooded the whole building.

Pushing all thoughts of possible failure aside, I fought my way through the icy water. Thankfully, Keira was keeping her cool despite this latest crazy development. Her SEAL father had probably taught her to swim, too. And she had already figured my plan as she scooped up my silver daggers and sidearm. Would the wet gun and submachine gun still work? I hoped they would. After all, they were magic.

I found my gauntlet, slipped it over my wrist, and snatched the glowing submachine gun. The light radiating from the weapon seemed to prove to me that its magic remained intact. Plus, it provided some light as we pushed our way through the submerged bedroom. Keira's framed photographs floated past me, torn from their proper place on the dresser by the instantaneous flooding of the apartment.

Rage filled my chest. Hadn't Keira been through enough? Did this bastard have to invade her home too?

I wanted to hurt the hovering mage outside the window. I would get my chance shortly.

Fueled by anger, I kept pushing out with my legs, while Keira expertly mirrored my moves. We powered through the dense mass of water, swimming side by side, and arrived in the apartment's living room. Chairs, cups, and lamps drifted through the flooded room, buoyed by the water. I almost expected Brogan to materialize in front of us like a shark ready to draw blood, but the mage was nowhere to be seen. He'd experienced first hand what I was capable of back in the Malibu mansion. Better to sit this one out and let us drown like rats. Who needed a direct confrontation when you could cut off someone's oxygen, right?

And talking about oxygen, or lack thereof, my lungs were starved for air. I had to break out of this death trap. Fast.

I kicked myself off the wall with both feet and shot like a torpedo toward the nearest living room window. Outside, the traffic twinkled, distorted by watery blur.

I touched the glass. There was no sign of Brogan. I guess he just liked peeping into bedrooms.

The next step of the plan seemed straightforward. Break the window and let the water rush outside. Despite my screaming lungs, I hesitated. A new thought had occurred to me. Would shattering the window create a whole new problem? Conceivably, it might depressurize the apartment and send Keira, myself, and hundreds of gallons of water through the window down to the street below. An eight-story drop would prove fatal.

After using up a precious second to think, I decided it

was worth the risk. I planned to hold on to the window sill with all my enhanced strength and stop us from being dragged outside if it came to that. I had no idea if it would work, but time was running out. Dark clouds were already forming in my field of vision. I had to act.

Tapping into all my strength, my fist blasted out at the window. The glass shattered, but nothing much else happened. The water refused to escape from the opening, almost as if some invisible wall was holding it in place.

Brogan's spell was even more powerful than I thought.

Fucking magic! What I wouldn't give for a nice RPG or a claymore mine. My military background was nearly useless in this war. This was a new fight with new rules. The Shadow Cabal's rules.

*You're not the man you once were*, I told myself. *You're the Night Slayer.*

My magic was depleted, and the agony in my lungs was becoming worse than the throbbing chest wound.

Desperate, I stuck my head out the window, and for one precious second, I was able to breathe. I toyed with the idea of climbing out, but there was no ledge and no way I could scale bare walls without plunging to my death within seconds. Plus, there was the matter of my new friend. Keira was still inside the apartment. And unlike me, she wasn't getting a chance to feed her starving lungs. I had to find another way out of the water-filled apartment. A better way.

I gorged on oxygen and pulled my head back inside. My darting gaze landed on the door leading out to the hallway. I glanced at Keira who was struggling, her gaze distant, and then pushed off from the window sill toward the door.

I shot over the couch and the ruined big screen TV. I zoomed past Keira, who was clinging to the wall with what little strength she had left as if it was a life preserver. Her eyes were wide and big with fear and pain, her agony etched into her features. Any second now, she would take in that first deep breath of water, and she would drown in front of my eyes.

No! I wouldn't let it happen. No one was going to die today except Brogan.

As soon as I reached the door, I flipped open the lock, snatched the door handle, and started pulling with all my strength. Naturally, the door didn't budge, the water pressure keeping it tightly sealed.

I wondered if Brogan was somehow following my desperate battle for survival. I could almost feel his gaze boring into me.

I clenched my jaw. One thing was becoming clear—brute force wouldn't open the door. Even if used my dragon blood and punched my way through the flimsy wood, Keira would never last that long. One final option remained.

*Magic.*

I swallowed the pain in my throbbing chest and turned inward. My magic was all but spent, but maybe I could tap into one last reservoir of power, just enough to blast my way through the closed door. I had to try.

I focused my mind, blocked everything else out. A stream of bubbles blew from lips, and I shot a glance at Keira. I saw the desperation on her lovely features.

Shit, she wasn't going to make it.

And for a moment, it felt like I was looking at Leah, my fellow SWAT officer. I blinked, and the eight other members of my team drifted through the apartment, rotting corpses suspended in a watery grave. Lifeless, bloated faces stared back at me with dark accusation. They had trusted me to keep them safe, but I let them down. Let them die. They were gone and buried, while I had cheated death. I could hear their incessant whispers in my head.

*Why keep fighting the inevitable? Why go on?*

I tightened my jaw, and my heart slammed against my chest.

The floating corpses of my team drew closer, their dangling arms reaching out for me...

No, I had survived for a reason. This was my chance to make things right. To avenge my fallen friends. To keep others safe.

Brogan must be triggering this horror show. He had gotten into my head somehow, found the images that would hurt me the most.

*Get the Hell out of my mind, you bastard!*

My blood boiled with righteous fury as I violently drew a circle in the water. My lips twisted into a snarl. The water started to heat up while the door in front of me turned a fiery red.

*Open fucking sesame!*

And then the wooden door incinerated in an explosive flash of magical energy. Blinding light enveloped the apartment and erased the dead SWAT members from view.

*I'm done with cheap magic tricks, Brogan, you hear me? I'm ready to face you man to man.*

For a surreal beat, I stared at the hallway beyond the apartment. Again, the water remained contained in Keira's unit, with not a single drop spilled.

I whirled toward Keira, who was swimming toward me with a last burst of strength. I dragged her with me over the threshold.

A beat later, we burst from the water-filled apartment and landed on the dry hallway floor, soaked to the bone and gasping for air. Keira collapsed and struggled to breathe, coughing up water. I leaned over her, ready to perform mouth-to-mouth if she needed it. She wheezed and choked but was breathing. Keira was a real fighter.

She was still gasping for precious oxygen when footsteps rang down the corridor. Brogan lurked at the far end, fronting an elevator door. I automatically stole a quick glance in the opposite direction and froze. The hallway stretched endlessly before me with no end in sight. Another magic trick. Brogan's message was quite clear. There would be no escape. I would have to go through him.

Honestly, I wouldn't have it any other way.

I turned back to my enemy. The succubus had wiped out my team, but in the end, the demon hadn't been much more than a ravenous animal. This power-hungry acolyte had set the gears in motion that ended up costing my friends' lives. This asshole was to blame.

The twin blades of my gauntlet snapped out with a loud *snick*. My other hand brought up my machine pistol.

Brogan smiled, secure in his powers.

Before I could squeeze off a round, gunfire filled the hallway. Behind me, Keira unloaded my sidearm into Brogan. The acolyte nonchalantly waved his hand in response, and with a sizzling hiss, a shield enveloped his whole body in a protective cocoon of magical energy. The silver bullets incinerated on contact.

I stole a glance at Keira. Recognized her frustration as she lowered her empty gun in defeat. Bullets wouldn't stop this agent of chaos.

Brogan began striding toward us with determined, measured steps. As the Cabal acolyte drew closer, he said, "Who are you? Your magic is pathetic, but someone must have taught you these parlor tricks."

"My parlor tricks were enough to blow up your little clubhouse."

Brogan flinched at my words. Encouraged by his subtle but unmistakable reaction, I continued to push those buttons. "I wonder what the Dark Masters will say when they discover that it was you who led me to the mansion."

Brogan eyed me with confusion. I looked nothing like the hipster student who had shaken his hand a day earlier. Time to jog the bastard's memory a bit.

I did my best impression of my College groupie voice. "Professor Brogan, my name is John. It's an honor to meet you. My friends have been bugging me to check out your class. I will definitely be enrolling next semester." I paused dramatically and explained, "I marked you with the Eye of Horus after you finished your lecture."

Shock rippled over Brogan's face as he grasped his role in what had happened. He studied his right hand, whispered words in a language I didn't understand, and the tracking symbol grew visible on his palm.

"Even if you deliver my head to your masters on a silver platter, they will blame you for what happened. An acolyte who became too cocky for his own good."

"They will understand. You tricked me."

"Of course." A wry smile crept across my lips. "They seem like an understanding bunch. I bet knowing you royally fucked up will do wonders for your future in their sick, power-hungry little club."

Brogan went pale. Good, I was getting under his skin. His magic might be better than mine, but my Kung Fu was stronger. I was doing my darnedest to even the playing field. All I had to do was bide my time, keep picking at him until he made a mistake.

I really thought I was gaining the upper hand. But that all changed when the skin on my chest distended and a wormlike creature slithered below my skin. I gasped, clawing at my chest.

Brogan regarded me with a widening smile. As his peals of laughter echoed through the passageway, I knew I was royally screwed.

## 17

Beads of sweat raced down my temples as the snakelike shape slithered underneath the skin of my pectoral muscle. There was only one explanation. The giant in the pit had infected me with some sort of parasite.

"Not a parasite, my foolish friend," Brogan said with a chuckle. "Offspring."

I glared at Brogan, realizing he had picked up my last thought. The worm wiggled beneath my skin, and I choked back a scream.

"I bet you didn't know the Nockmars are hermaphrodites, capable of fertilizing both females and males. How do you feel about becoming a proud papa?"

I gnashed my teeth, rage making me momentarily forget the pain. Man, how I wished to wipe that shit-eating grin off his ugly mug.

Brogan inexorably closed in, a predator zeroing in on his prey for the kill, indifferent to the glowing submachine gun in my hand. He started walking sideways and up the wall like a spider, unaffected by gravity. Within seconds he had reached the ceiling and now advanced upside down.

The fucker was showing off his bag of tricks, demonstrating his superiority. I flashed back to my first encounter with the succubus inside the downtown apartment building. She too had shown a preference for walking on ceilings. It had to be a Cabal thing. I almost chuckled at my dark sense of humor, but the crawling pain in my chest kept the smile off my face.

As the creature stirred inside of me, another realization hit me. I knew how Brogan had found me. He must've homed in on the parasite's magical signature. Nockmar Jr. had led the fiend straight to us.

"I picked up another voice in your head," Brogan said. "Who were you talking to? I bet it was the same person who taught you spell craft and provided you with these toys. Who dares turn against the Cabal?"

The question hung in the air. Brogan had another thing coming if he thought I was going to give up the sorceress to save my own skin.

"Talk to me, Jason. Tell me who you're working with."

"Go fuck yourself!"

Irritation flickered in Brogan's eyes, but he kept his cool. "I won't lie to you. There is no chance that I'll spare you. But I can promise you a swift, painless death if you answer a few questions. If you refuse to help, the alternative will be far less pleasant. The creature inside of you is growing. As it gains size, it will grow hungrier and devour you from the inside like cancer. First your muscle tissue, then the organs. This will be a slow, agonizing gestation. The creature knows which organs to avoid and which you can survive without for a short while. It's programmed to keep its host alive for as long as possible. Once you are skin and bones, it will finally put you out of your misery. But by then you will have gone mad with pain."

I bit my lips. I could almost feel the parasite clawing into my muscles, nibbling away at my strength.

"It's over. Time to share your secrets."

Through a haze of agony, I mentally ran down my list of options. I could empty my weapon into Brogan, but then what? If he deflected the bullets again, it would come down to my gauntlet and daggers. What chance did those weapons stand? And could I even manage hand-to-hand combat with a fucking nightmare worm in my chest?

I stole a glance at Keira. She stood a few feet behind me, rooted to the spot, her finger closed around one of my silver daggers as if it was a protective talisman. The blessed knife wouldn't do much good against Brogan's magic.

*I'm so sorry*, I thought. *I tried to save you. I really did.*

Frustration detonated inside of me. Octurna had been right. I wasn't ready to go up against the Cabal. It appeared the Midnight War would be over before it had a chance to even get started.

Another spasm erupted in my chest, and I hunched over, struggling for air. The pain was unbearable. I had become a living incubator for a monster. I tried to think of a worse way to die, but nothing came to mind.

"It's too bad you won't be alive to see the birth of your child, Jason. I wonder if he takes after his dad or his *dad*."

Brogan's sardonic laughter rang out, and I would've given up my left nut to ram my fist into that smirking face.

I blearily looked down the hallway and saw the elevator door open. Despite my suffering, knowing some innocent was about to emerge from the lift and step right into this nightmare made me mad. Another person would perish because of my failure to stop this monster.

*"Stop beating yourself up, Jason."*

My heart skipped a beat when I recognized the person in the open elevator. It was Octurna. Her red robe billowed around her as if she was at the center of a storm, her regal features inspiring devotion. Had she set foot in the world, knowing she would succumb to the Cabal's death spell? I caught a glimpse of the black throne behind her, the space inside the elevator eerily elongated.

Holy Shit, Octurna had materialized the Sanctuary inside the Keira's apartment building! The elevator had become the portal to the fortress.

*"Bring this dog to me, Slayer."*

It sounded so simple. All I had to do was push Brogan into the waiting elevator. Once inside the fortress, Octurna could turn her magic against the bastard. And despite his powers, I knew he was no match for the sorceress, even in her weakened state.

Only about fifteen feet separated Brogan from the elevator, but it might as well have been a mile in my current condition.

*I've got nothing left,* I thought. *Sorry, boss.*

*"The creature inside of you has fed on your dragon blood. It's tainted by your magic. And that makes the creature yours to command. Make the parasite do your bidding!"*

Octurna's cryptic command came to me through a cloud of pain. What was the sorceress talking about? How could I control the slithering beast inside of me? And how could that help me, anyway?

I saw the worm snake underneath my abdominal wall and almost gagged. And then an idea hit me. It was crazy, most likely doomed to failure, but dammit, it was also worth a shot.

As Brogan appeared above me and flipped from the ceiling back the floor, I focused on the nasty bugger wiggling around in my torso. I tried to visualize the thing outlined beneath my skin. At first, nothing happened, and then, like a faint echo, I heard a hiss. The parasite was not happy about my attempts to control its motor functions. It struggled, resisted, and then succumbed to my will.

*That's right, buddy, who is in charge now?*

The thrashing under my skin stopped, and the creature began to push against my skin instead of trying to burrow deeper into the muscle tissue. It wasn't ready yet to emerge from his warm host. It still had so much more feeding to do, but the power of the Dragon Blood wasn't leaving it a choice.

Brogan stepped in front of me, features twisted in an expression of triumph.

"So what will it be? A slow or a quick death?'

"You tell me, asshole."

And with these words, I gave the parasite inside my chest a mental push. If you've seen *Alien*, you have a good idea what happened next.

The serpentine parasite, all twelve inches of its gore-streaked albino form, erupted from my skin and shot out like a living arrow right at Brogan's shocked face. The creature's tiny, hungry head, topped with a ring of sharp, blood-stained teeth, buried itself into Brogan's neck before he could ignite his protective shield. As he staggered back with a scream, I brought up my rune-engraved machine pistol and let loose, each bullet tearing into the Cabal's lackey.

His shield crackled weakly around him, his mind occupied with keeping the parasite from tearing his face off. The shield stopped the bullets but failed to incinerate them. The impact of each projectile hitting the shield pushed him down the hallway toward the waiting elevator.

Octurna meanwhile had vanished in the lift's shadows, but I knew she was lurking in the darkness. Waiting for Brogan to enter a realm where she made the rules.

But first this asshole would have to cross the threshold.

Blood gushing from the hole the parasite had torn through my body, I staggered to my feet, weapon leveled, and stumbled forward while I kept blasting away at Brogan like a maniac.

He had almost reached the elevator when Brogan tore the screeching parasite into two bloody, ragged halves. The severed parts of the dead creature hit the hallway's faded carpet. Brogan stood at the edge at the elevator, eyes squirming with mad rage, his face streaked with blood from the bites of the parasite. At the same time, my sub gun stopped firing, the mag empty now. And there was no time to reload.

With a primal war cry, I launched myself at the fiend, the twin blades of my gauntlet out. I barreled into Brogan's shield, which felt like hitting a brick wall. And even though the shell of energy had stopped me cold, Brogan had instinctively backed away from the gore-streaked berserker determined to kill him. He stumbled back and…

Crossed the elevator's threshold.

*Gotcha!*

With savage glee, I dove into the elevator after my enemy.

I arrived inside the Sanctuary's observation chamber.

*Home sweet home.*

A stunned, incredulous Brogan took in his transformed surroundings, clearly not quite sure what had happened and where he was.

Behind me, I saw a stunned Keira staring back at me from the hallway before the elevator door transformed into a stained-glass window, reducing her to a frozen, painted image on the sparkling glass.

I pivoted back to Brogan. He glared at me and lobbed a fearsome ball of energy at me. The impact sent me flying, and I landed right on top of the display stand that held the succubus' skull. The trophy went flying as I crashed to the ground.

I tried to get back to my feet, but my muscles refused to respond. There was only so much punishment I could take.

I was out for the count. Time for Octurna to make her move—but where the hell was the sorceress?

Brogan stalked toward me, eyes alight with unbridled hatred. He looked insane, his once-handsome face a bloody, ruined mask. One thing was for sure, the professor wouldn't be seducing young coeds any time soon. He took in his alien surroundings, studied in the wall of stained-glass, the black throne that jutted from the ground like a broken tooth, the displays cases full of ominous monster skulls.

"Where the fuck am I?"

Octurna's icy voice answered from the chamber's shadows. "This is your last stop on the way to Hell, Brogan. Enjoy the sights while you can."

The sorceress' disembodied presence made Brogan whirl around.

"Show yourself. You think this smoke and mirror bullshit scares me? Do you know who I am? What I'm capable of?"

"Of course. You are the first mage to fall in the coming war. Your head will make a lovely addition to my collection."

Brogan regarded the skulls and traded a terrified look with me.

Octurna's laugh echoed through the shadows. "You wanted to learn magic, master the mysteries of the universe, be part of the coming darkness. Everything comes at a price."

"Shut the fuck up!"

"How many innocents perished in your mad, selfish quest for power? How many will get to live once you're gone from this world?"

"You can't scare me! I serve the Seven!"

"No, you serve me!"

Octurna's voice hummed with fierce intensity. Fuck, a shiver was even spiking up my spine.

And as if to prove her point, the skin on Brogan's face and body began to bubble and grow waxy. Horror rippled over his features as they started to melt like a human candle.

"No, no, no…"

His heaving voice echoed through the observation chamber as his legs collapsed in a puddle and his torso liquefied into a bloody mess before my eyes. Skin streamed down his face in sheets. He deserved on every level what was happening to him, but I couldn't help but feel terror as I bore witness to his gruesome fate.

"Help. Me," he said in a gurgling voice. To my horror, Brogan was still alive, more than half of his body reduced to viscous, sticky goo. Octurna's fearsome magic was drawing out the fiend's exit from this planet.

"You are the first of my enemies to fall, Brogan," Octurna said. "Your dark masters and their monstrous servants will soon follow."

"They will…destroy…," he stammered weakly. The words died on his lips as his mouth collapsed like a block of melting cheese.

Octurna peeled from the shadows. She stood like an avenging angel of death over the expanding puddle of red at her feet. Her beautiful face severe, her jet-black hair framing her features like a dark halo, red dress billowing seductively around her tall frame. I saw the delicate network of her tattoos ignite as she absorbed Brogan's magical energy. There was something both chilling and seductive about the joy she took in vanquishing her enemy.

Our gazes met across the chamber, and a smile lit up those mysterious, otherworldly features. The sorceress offered me her hand and lifted me back to my feet. The wound in my chest closed and my tats shimmered as Octurna shared some of her newly absorbed power with me. My strength returned.

Octurna leaned closer, and before I knew what was happening, she planted a quick kiss on my cheek. "You did well, Slayer."

She turned back to the puddle of melted flesh and bone and held up her hand. The puddle stirred, and a round object shot from remains and landed in the palm of her right hand. She proudly held the blood-covered object up at me. It was Brogan's skull, the last bits of melted skin evaporating from the bone in a scarlet puff. With an air of grave ceremony, she placed our dead enemy's skull on the nearest display case, adding Brogan to her rapidly expanding macabre collection.

"At this rate, you may need a bigger trophy room," I deadpanned.

A devilish grin flickered over her stunning features. "I certainly hope so."

I smiled despite myself. The sorceress was a piece of work. But so was I.

I walked up to the stained-glass windows, watched as the colored glass became glimpses of reality as I drew closer. I searched the tapestry of windows, looking for the woman I left behind on Earth. I spotted Keira within seconds. She was inside the elevator. It had long ceased to be a doorway to another world. Incomprehension and concern filled her face. I wanted to tell her she shouldn't worry, that everything was okay.

Octurna appeared next to me. "She made an impression on both of us. Brave, beautiful and smart. Plus, her ties to the press could prove useful. Why don't you go to her now?"

I held Octurna's gaze, surprised by her generous gesture. I cherished the moments I'd shared with Keira, but every time I looked at Octurna, I couldn't help but think about our first heated encounter. Would there ever be a repeat performance? Did I even *want* one, knowing what I did about the ageless, bloodthirsty warrior-queen beside me?

Hell if I know.

"Okay," I finally said. "And...thanks."

The window showing Keira expanded, turning into a doorway to Earth.

"Go. Spent the night in her warm embrace. Tomorrow we continue your training."

I nodded, knowing that many challenges lay ahead. My gaze lingered on Octurna, and I took a step toward her, emboldened by her earlier kiss. Recognizing the desire in my eyes, she shook her head and placed a hand on my chest, gently pushing me away.

I pulled back, disappointed. The sorceress regarded me, her features turning severe.

"Believe me, Jason, we make better partners than lovers.

I sighed. "I know."

Was I being honest with myself? Not according to the lingering memory of our first—and only—time together.

I took a step toward the window. Toward a woman who was brave and kind, and a hell of a good shot. Keira was nothing like Octurna. But maybe that's exactly what I needed right now.

"Hey, whatever happens in the next few hours, don't spy on us," I said.

"You ask a lot, Slayer." Octurna said with a playful twinkle in her eye.

I smiled back at her.

I stepped through the window and appeared in the apartment hallway. Keira had almost reached her door, her back turned to me. I stole a final glance at the elevator where Octurna stood. There was a trace of longing in those beautiful eyes. It struck me how incredibly lonely Octurna must be. I felt torn. Part of me wanted to return to the Sanctuary. But she'd made it clear that I wouldn't be welcome in her bed, in her heart.

At least not yet.

And then the elevator door closed, erasing the sorceress from view. Up ahead, Keira responded to the sound, her eyes going wide when she spotted me. She rushed toward me, face glowing with relief. The feel of her arms around me pushed all other thoughts aside.

I scooped Keira into my arms.

I was no fool. Life would not be the same after what had happened in Malibu. I had fired the first shot in a new war. Dark days lay ahead, but tonight I would cast all fears of the uncertain future aside and remind myself why men fight wars in the first place.

The world was a beautiful place. It was worth dying for—but it was worth living for, too.

And with this thought, I crossed the threshold of Keira's apartment, lost in her warm embrace.

THE END

**Jason Night returns in**

**Monster Quest**

**Available Now!**

Thank you for reading NIGHT SLAYER: MIDNIGHT WAR. Please help out and leave a review.

Quick and Easy Review Link!

More Books are coming soon. Visit amazon.com/author/williammassa and press "**FOLLOW**" to be automatically notified of future releases.
The best is yet to come.

**Want to get an email when the next NIGHT SLAYER title is released, learn about deals and receive a free supernatural novella? Subscribe to my newsletter!**

Click here to get started!

Many thanks to the **Harem Lit Facebook** group for fostering a sense of community for this fun new genre. Visit the group and comment on your favorite titles.

**Come join the discussion!**

## ALSO BY WILLIAM MASSA

### THE NIGHT SLAYER SERIES

Midnight War

Monster Quest

Shadow Plague

### THE SHADOW DETECTIVE SERIES

Cursed City

Soul Catcher

Blood Rain

Demon Dawn

Skull Master

Ghoul Night

Witch Wars

Crimson Circle

Hell Breaker

Dragon Curse (coming in 2019)

### THE OCCULT ASSASSIN SERIES

Damnation Code

Apocalypse Soldier

Spirit Breaker

Soul Jacker

Black Sun (coming in 2019)

Doomsday Circle (coming in 2019)

## THE GARGOYLE KNIGHT SERIES

Gargoyle Knight

Gargoyle Quest

## STAND ALONES

Fear the Light

## ABOUT THE AUTHOR

William Massa is a produced screenwriter and bestselling Amazon author. His film credits include *Return to House on Haunted Hill* and he has sold pitches and scripts to Warner, USA TV, Silver Pictures, Dark Castle, Maverick and Sony.

William has lived in New York, Florida, Europe and now resides in Venice Beach surrounded by skaters and surfers. He writes science fiction and dark fantasy/urban fantasy horror with an action-adventure flavor.

Writing can be a solitary pursuit but rewriting can be a

group effort. I strive to make each book better than the last and feedback is incredibly helpful. If you have notes, thoughts or comments about this book or want to contact me, feel free to contact me at:

williammassabooks@gmail.com

Hope to hear from you soon!

Printed in Great Britain
by Amazon